THERE'S A COW IN MY SWIMMING POOL

Other Scholastic books by Martyn Godfrey:

Monsters in the School
I Spent My Summer Vacation Kidnapped Into Space
Here She Is, Ms. Teeny-Wonderful
It Isn't Easy Being Ms. Teeny-Wonderful
Send in Ms. Teeny-Wonderful
Alien Wargames
The Day the Sky Exploded

THERE'S A COW IN MY SWIMMING POOL

MARTYN GODFREY : FRANK O'KEEFFE

Cover by
Brian Boyd

Scholastic Canada Ltd.

Scholastic Canada Ltd.
123 Newkirk Road, Richmond Hill, Ontario, Canada L4C 3G5

Scholastic Inc.
730 Broadway, New York, NY 10003, USA

Ashton Scholastic Limited
Private Bag 1, Penrose, Auckland, New Zealand

Ashton Scholastic Pty Limited
PO Box 579, Gosford, NSW 2250, Australia

Scholastic Publications Ltd.
Holly Walk, Leamington Spa, Warwickshire CV32 4LS, England

Canadian Cataloguing in Publication Data

Godfrey, Martyn
There's a cow in my swimming pool

ISBN 0-590-74045-8

I. O'Keeffe, Frank. II. Title.

PS8563.034T5 1991 jC813'.54 C9094302-8
PZ7.G6Th 1991

6 5 4 3 2 1 Printed in Canada 1 2 3 4 5/9
Manufactured by Gagné Printing

Contents

To the "cool, crazy" critics in Mr. Fitz's sixth grade class, Keeno School, St. Albert, 1991

1

I Feel Weird

I sat on the end of my bed and slipped on my white high-heeled shoes. "I feel weird, Robyn," I confessed. "It's finally happening, and I don't like it."

My best friend, Robyn Baker, studied herself in my full-length bedroom mirror. "Maybe we should have picked blue dresses," she said. "This pink makes my hair and freckles look even redder."

"I guess I have every right to feel strange," I went on. "How many kids get to be a bridesmaid at their mom's wedding? How many kids have their old fifth grade teacher as their new stepdad?"

"Do you think I've put on too much mascara, Nicole?" Robyn asked.

"Why don't you ever listen to me?" I complained. "Whenever I tell you something serious, you never listen. I said the wedding makes me feel weird."

Robyn faced me and smiled. "Well, you don't look weird. The pink dress is perfect on you. Your hair is great with the curls. You should get it permed so it looks that way all the time."

I sighed in frustration. I should know better than to try to discuss my feelings with Robyn. Especially when she was so excited about being a bridesmaid.

I stood up and stared at my reflection in the mirror, checking my browny-blonde hair, my long bridesmaid dress and my shiny shoes.

Why aren't I feeling happy? I wondered. I should be feeling happy.

"It's so different to see you dressed up," Robyn said. "I'm used to seeing you in jeans and a T-shirt."

"We look like teenagers," I noted.

Robyn grinned. "Great, huh? Being twelve is almost the same thing as being a teenager anyway. You know, it's too bad all this is wasted. There aren't going to be any boys at the wedding to see us. How come you don't have any thirteen-year-old cousins? How come Mr. Manning doesn't have any thirteen-year-old nephews?"

"Barry," I corrected. "Mr. Manning wants us to call him Barry."

And that's weird too, I thought. Calling my old teacher by his first name. Having him move to the farm with Mom and me. Becoming an official part of our family.

I remembered back to when Mom met my soon-to-be stepdad, Barry Manning. It was at the first parent-teacher interview in fifth grade.

Dad had been dead for two years then. Mom and I sat at Mr. Manning's desk as he explained how well I was doing in math and how my reading and writing were okay, but I could improve if I didn't try to finish so quickly. Then he talked about himself. I remember wondering about that — why he did it — at the time.

He told Mom how he'd grown up in Edmonton but had always loved the forests of western Alberta, and how he'd jumped at the opportunity to teach in Picture Rapids and how the town was so pretty, being in the foothills with the mountains only a few kilometers away — and so on.

And Mom told him how she'd grown up in Medicine Hat, how she'd met Dad in college, got married and moved to a farm outside of town, about me, Nicole Ashley Rachel, being an only child, how we had some land cleared with over a hundred head of cattle and another part still bush, and how my father had been killed in a car accident — and so on.

All this at the first parent-teacher interview of

the year! I should have known Mom was making a special friend. Over the next few months, their friendship turned to love. And in two hours they'd be married and my life was going to be changed forever — again.

It changed the first time the day the stone-faced RCMP officer knocked on our door and said, "Mrs. Peters, I'm afraid I have some bad news . . . "

Robyn interrupted my thoughts. "I hope nothing goes wrong at the wedding."

"Wrong? What can go wrong?" I asked.

"Lots of stuff," she said. "I was reading in *Tattle Tale* the other day about weddings that turned out to be total disasters."

"*Tattle Tale*? That's one of those stupid magazines you buy at the supermarket checkout. None of that stuff is true. It's all made up."

"Is not," she said quickly. "It's all true. Why would they print it if it wasn't?"

"To make money from stupid people like you. I saw one in Safeway last week that said a boy was kidnapped by porcupines and grew up with quills all over his back. Do you really believe that?"

"So it sounds a little far-out," she admitted. "But who's to say it's not true?"

I laughed. "And I saw another headline that said a man had given birth to triplets."

"That's only three kids," she countered. "What's so unusual about that? I think the record is seven."

"A *man*," I repeated.

"You have to keep an open mind," Robyn said. "Anyway, I know the wedding disasters were real."

I shook my head. "I doubt it. They were probably made up too."

"There was a picture of one," she said. "So it had to be true. This bride arrived at church and got out of the car. She had on a beautiful white gown. When the car pulled away, her dress was caught in the door and it got ripped right off. She was left standing in her underwear in front of the church, holding her bouquet."

"There was a picture of that?"

"In color."

"That still doesn't mean it's real. The photo was probably fake. Anyway, my mom isn't going to be wearing a fancy dress. She has a yellow one that's really plain."

"In another story the groom's shoes blew up," Robin continued. "And in another, the ghost of Elvis . . ."

I didn't let her finish. "I'm not really interested in wedding stories from *Tattle Tale*."

Robyn quickly changed gear. "Are you interested in talking about what we're going to do after the wedding? I mean, I'm looking forward to you staying with me in town while your mom and Barry are on their honeymoon. What are we going to do for fun?"

"Whatever you want," I said. "The only thing I have to do is bike back to the farm every day and collect the eggs and feed the chickens."

"You don't have to take care of the bees or feed the cows?"

I shook my head. "I told you this already. Don't you listen to anything I tell you?"

"Tell me again."

"We only have one hive in the hayfield this year. I don't have to do anything about that. And the cattle are summer grazing in the pasture. I just check them to see if they're okay."

"What if they're not okay?"

"Then I call the vet or tell Mr. Stevens, our neighbor."

"And your grandpa isn't staying to help out because of his health?"

"That's what Mom says," I told her. "She doesn't want him working too hard. What's dumb about it is that he wants to go back to the Hat as soon as possible to play golf. Isn't playing golf the same as working?"

Robyn didn't bother to answer my question.

"What about your Aunt Alicia and Uncle Anwar?"

"They're driving in from Edmonton today. And they're going to drive back after the reception tonight."

"So we'll have your place all to ourselves, and all we're going to do is feed a bunch of chickens and check cows?"

"We can go swimming in my pool," I suggested.

"That's all right for a half-hour."

"We can go roller-skating," I said.

"Boring," she grumbled.

"Bowling?"

"Get serious, Nicole. Double boring."

"We can volunteer to help out at the daycare center."

"I don't want to spend time with little kids. Triple boring."

"We can go to the library and sign out a summer's worth of novels."

"Boring. Boring. Boring. Boring!" Robyn affirmed.

"Well, what do you have in mind?"

A sly smile crossed her face. "Like I said, we're going to have your farm to ourselves for a whole week, right? And we certainly don't want to hang around my house, do we? My sister is too bossy."

"What are you getting at?" I asked cautiously.

"This is the start of summer vacation. We've got to plan a party. Ask some friends out to swim in your pool. Some boys."

I thought about that. "It sounds like a great idea, but I'd better check with my mom first."

"Why do you have to say anything? She can't say no if you don't tell her."

"Because I always tell Mom what I'm doing," I said. "You know that. Anyway, I think she'll say yes. Kids come out to use the pool all the time. And if I'm responsible enough to take care of the farm while they're away, I should be responsible enough to have a party by myself. She's been making a big deal of the fact I'm going into junior high next fall."

"Right," Robyn agreed. "We're in seventh grade now. We're responsible. And your mom knows everyone in our class. Go ask her now, before she gets too busy with the wedding stuff."

"Okay," I said. "There's something I want to talk to her about anyway."

I left Robyn in my room fussing with her hair and knocked on Mom's door. She answered with a lyrical "come in" which told me how happy she was.

She was dressed in her robe, combing her long, blonde hair into a ponytail. She glanced at me. "Oh my!" She pretended to be shocked. "Who is this stranger in my house?"

"How do I look?" I asked.

"You look . . . you look wonderful, Nicole," she beamed. "And you make me feel old. I am simply too young to have a grown-up daughter."

I flashed my braces at her and she smiled back. "Are you and Robyn all dressed?"

I nodded and then tapped my watch. "Have you got time to talk?"

"Of course. You know how fast I can get dressed. I'll be ready when Grandpa comes back from town to pick us up. I just hope your Aunt Alicia gets her family ready on time. She's always late. I wish they'd come last night instead of driving from Edmonton today. I could have kept an eye on them."

As Mom tied back her hair, I thought about how beautiful she was. I hope I look like her when I grow up. Lots of people tell us we look alike.

"Maybe you should have gone to the hairdresser with me," I suggested. "Somehow it doesn't seem right to get married in a ponytail."

She shot me a give-me-a-break look.

I pointed at her wedding dress spread out on the bed. "And I'm not sure about your dress. People don't get married in yellow. It should be white."

"They don't wear white for their second wedding."

"Your nose is all sunburnt. It's really red," I continued. "You need to put lots of foundation on it."

"What's with you?" she asked. "Is this what you wanted to talk about?"

I shook my head. "It's about Mr. Manning . . . "

"Barry," Mom said.

"It's about Barry," I went on. "For a long time I've been feeling mixed up about him and I haven't wanted to say anything because I thought you'd get upset and I thought I'd get used to the idea as the wedding got closer and you were so happy and I didn't want to spoil that and I figured —"

"Whoa," Mom said. "Slow down, Nicole. What are you trying to say?"

I took a deep breath. "I feel sort of . . . sort of nervous about you marrying Mr. Man . . . I mean, Barry. I'm not sure I like the idea."

Mom put the brush down, turned around and took my hands in hers. "This is an odd time to be telling me this. How come you haven't said anything before? I thought you were looking forward to Barry sharing our lives."

"I thought I was," I tried to explain. "I really liked Barry as my teacher. And when you two got serious, I wanted to be happy because you were so happy. But even though I wanted it to feel right, truth is, it doesn't. I don't think I want things to change. I want it to be just you and me and the cows."

Mom smiled sympathetically.

"You're not mad at me for saying that?" I asked. "Especially now? I thought about keeping it a secret. But I just had to tell you."

Mom shook her head. "Of course I'm not angry. I'm glad you can talk honestly to me, even if you pick the most inconvenient time to do it. I wish you'd told me sooner. We should have discussed this a long time ago."

"I thought it would go away."

"At least this explains why you've been so cool to Barry. He's noticed, you know. He thinks you've been avoiding him."

"I didn't want to be rude."

She squeezed my hands. "I think what you're feeling is perfectly normal, honey. It's natural to worry about changes."

"I keep thinking about Dad," I told her. "Barry is so different from Dad. It won't be the same. And what if . . . " Suddenly my cheeks were awash with hot, streaming tears. "I remember him so well," I sobbed. "I remember how Dad smelled when he came in from his chores, like cows and hay and sweat. And I . . . I still miss him, Mom. Why did he leave us? Why did he go away when we needed him?"

Mom pulled me against her and hugged me so tightly that it hurt. I felt her chest heave as she fought back her own tears.

We stayed in that uncomfortable clinch for a minute, maybe longer. Finally, Mom gently pushed me away and grabbed a handful of Kleenex to wipe the wetness off my cheeks. "Enough of this. Weddings are happy times. We don't want to arrive at the church with puffy red eyes, do we? Let's think happy thoughts. And don't worry about anything, Nicole. Everything will be fine. Trust me. Everything will be fine."

I wanted to believe that. I really did.

2

The Wedding

Mom dabbed the last of the tears off my cheeks. "Are we feeling better now?"

"Yes," I lied.

"We'll talk more after Barry and I come home from the honeymoon. I promise."

I sucked in a mighty sniff to clear my nose.

"That's a disgusting noise," Mom declared.

"Sorry," I said. "There's one more thing."

"Can't it wait?" she sighed. "This is not the time for such heavy topics."

"This has nothing to do with Barry. It's just that Robyn and I want to invite a few people to use the pool next week, and I thought I should check it out with you."

"A few people?" she asked.

"Kids," I explained. "From school."

Mom thought for a moment. "These few people, would some of them be boys?"

"Just the guys from my class."

Again, Mom spent five seconds in thought. "So you want to have a pool party?"

I shook my head. "Not really a party. Just some friends for a swim."

"It sounds like a pool party to me. And I'm not sure I like the idea."

"Why?" I wondered. "I'm in seventh grade now. I'm responsible."

"You'll be in seventh grade in September," she pointed out. "And yes, you're responsible enough to check on the farm. And you're responsible enough to stay at Robyn's house for a week. But I'd be worried there could be an accident in the pool."

"Mom, it's an above-ground pool. It's barely a meter deep all over. Nothing is going to happen. My friends come out to visit and swim all the time."

"Yes," she agreed. "But I'm around those times."

"Some of the time you're around. And some of the time you're out in the pasture. And some of the time you're in town."

"It's not just the worry about someone being hurt, it's . . . " She paused as if she was having trouble finding the right words. " . . . it's just that girls your age don't have parties with boys without an adult around."

"Why not?"

"It just isn't done."

"Give me a break, Mom. What do you think is going to happen?"

"Well . . . " She blushed slightly.

"Get real," I groaned. "Do think it's going to be a make-out party?"

Her blush deepened.

"Where would you get such a dumb idea?"

"I don't appreciate your tone of voice," she scolded. "Just the fact that you know what that is shows me I have every right to be concerned."

I shook my head in disbelief. "That really is stupid, Mom. Honest."

"Still . . . "

"Look, a couple of minutes ago, you asked me to trust you about Barry. Now I'm asking you to trust me about this."

Mom spent another short time in thought. "All right," she said reluctantly. "I'll trust you. But you have to promise it'll be no more than a few people. I'll be upset if I find out you've had a crowd out here."

"A deal," I said. "Thanks."

We heard Grandpa's old Buick rumble into our driveway.

Mom glanced at her watch. "Is Dad back from the barber already? I do have to hurry."

✦ ✦ ✦

Robyn and I sat in the back seat for the short ride into town. Mom spent the drive nagging her father about the stale tobacco smell in his car. "I wish you'd stop smoking, Dad. I worry about you. First, I lost Mom. Then Steve. I don't want to lose you. You've already had one heart attack."

"A minor one," Grandpa argued.

"If you ask me, there's no such thing as a *minor* heart attack," Mom countered. "Why don't you do what the doctor told you?"

"My doctor," Grandpa grumbled. "If I followed her advice I'd have nothing left to live for."

"She told you to quit smoking," Mom went on.

"I've cut back," he said defensively.

"She told you to give up fatty foods. I noticed how much butter you spread on your toast this morning."

"I've cut back."

"She told you to stop eating salt. You sure poured a lot on your eggs at breakfast."

"I've cut back on that too."

"You have to stop, Dad. Not simply cut back."

Grandpa winked at Mom. "The doctor told me that playing golf was good for me, and I'm following that advice."

Robyn poked me in the ribs. "You okay, Nicole? You're all quiet."

"I'm just thinking," I told her.

Despite Mom's assurance, I was far from convinced the marriage was going to be a good thing. It was just too big a change. Mom was right, I should have said something a long time ago. Why had I thought the doubtful feelings would go away?

✦ ✦ ✦

Reverend Slipstead's car was the only one in the church parking lot when we arrived.

"Good," Mom declared. "We're on time. Let's get inside. People will arrive any minute. I hope Alicia gets here before the whole thing's over."

As we got out of the car, I noticed Sammy Kirkus walking down the sidewalk. Sammy was in my sixth grade class. I don't like him because he seems to go out of his way to give me a hard time. But it wasn't Sammy I was interested in right then. It was the boy walking with him who caught my attention.

Robyn was watching the stranger too. "Who's that?" she whispered.

"I don't know," I whispered back.

"He's gorgeous. Let's go find out." Then she said

to my mother, "You go ahead, Mrs. P. We just want to say hello to our friends."

"All right," Mom nodded. "But only for a few seconds."

"Hey, it's Dopey and Dippy," Sammy said as we walked across the lawn toward him. "How come you're all dressed up stupid? You entering the Ms. Teeny-Wonderful contest?"

"You know Nicole's mom is marrying Mr. Manning today," Robyn snarled. "Or are you so dumb that you forgot?"

"I remembered," Sammy snarled back. Then he turned to the stranger. "Brent, meet two of the goofiest girls in town."

"Hi," Robyn said to Brent. "You're gorgeous."

How could she say stuff like that, even if it was true? Brent had long wavy brown hair and deep, soft, brown eyes.

He seemed confused by Robyn's comment. "I'm Brent McGregor," he said. "I just moved to town today. Sammy is showing me around."

"Great," Robyn said. "It's about time we had a good-looking boy in Picture Rapids."

"I'm Nicole Peters," I said to Brent. "Glad to meet you."

To my surprise, he shook my hand. His hand was warm and soft and strong, and like a lot of things that were happening to me that day, holding it made me feel really weird.

Robyn grabbed his hand after me. "I'm Robyn Baker. You want to get married? Maybe Reverend Slipstead will do two for the price of one."

"Robyn!" I said.

"He knows I'm kidding. Look, Brent, if you get tired of having stupid Sammy show you around, give me a call. My number is 555-1213. I'd love to give you a grand tour of Picture Rapids."

Brent looked more puzzled.

"Nicole, Robyn," Grandpa called from the church steps. "Aunt Alicia is here. We're wanted in the Reverend's office."

"We have to go," I said.

Brent smiled at me. Two little dimples appeared on his cheeks. "It was nice meeting you."

"See you around," I said.

"555-1213," Robyn repeated. "Call me anytime. Day or night."

As we walked back to the church, I said, "How can you say those things without being embarrassed?"

She shrugged. "He won't call. I can tell."

"After the way you behaved, he probably thinks you're crazy."

"Not because of that," Robyn told me. "He won't

call me because he likes you."

"What?"

"He likes you. Couldn't you tell? Didn't you notice the way he was looking at you?"

✦ ✦ ✦

Robyn's observation didn't help me feel any less weird. I spent the entire wedding with bizarre thoughts zapping through my head.

As the organ played the wedding march, Grandpa led Mom up the aisle. Aunt Alicia was behind them. Robyn and I walked side by side behind her. Everyone in the church turned to look at Mom and us.

This is dumb, I thought.

Then the ceremony started. When the minister asked, "Who gives this woman?" Grandpa proudly said, "I do," and passed Mom's hand to Mr. Manning.

I wondered why women had to be given away by their fathers. How come guys don't have to be given away by their mothers?

There's no way Mr. Manning or anybody else is going to give me away at my wedding, I thought. I'll go because I want to.

I watched Mom as she repeated the words she had to say after the pastor. Her ponytail looks funny, I thought. So does her lemon yellow dress.

Even if it is her second time, she should wear white.

Mr. Manning repeated his words.

He sounds nervous, I thought. Maybe he's having second thoughts. Maybe he'll change his mind.

He didn't.

The pastor said, "I now pronounce you husband and wife."

Mom looked so beautiful. Even if her nose was too red.

I glanced over at Robyn. She was staring at Mom and Mr. Manning as they kissed. She looked starry-eyed and dreamy.

All I could think was, My fifth grade teacher is kissing my mother. They kissed for a long time.

Gross!

The organ played loudly. Another thought popped into my head. I'm probably going to have a dopey baby brother nine months from now.

Then, while everyone else was leaving the church, the happy couple went with Reverend Slipstead to sign some stuff.

✦ ✦ ✦

Ten minutes later, Mom and Mr. Manning reappeared on the steps and were attacked by guests throwing birdseed.

Birdseed was Mr. Manning's idea. He's into the

environment. "Confetti wastes paper and leaves garbage on the ground," he lectured over supper one day when he and Mom were planning the wedding. "We'll insist the guests throw birdseed. That way we'll feed our feathered friends after the celebration."

What a dumb idea, I thought now, even though it had struck me as a good one when I first heard it.

Robyn gave me a handful. I threw it, and a bunch of tiny seeds landed on Mr. Manning's bald spot, which is where I was aiming.

For a half-hour after that, people stood around on the church lawn talking and congratulating the newlyweds. At one point we had to pose for photographs.

The photographers took all kinds of pictures — me with Mom, me with Mr. Manning, me with Robyn, me with Mom and Aunt Alicia.

I was embarrassed when the photographer snapped a picture while I was behind Mom and Mr. Manning brushing the dust off my white shoes.

"That'll be a cute one," Robyn teased. "The bride and groom smiling happily while you stick your bum in the air."

✦ ✦ ✦

Just as everybody was getting into their cars to head for the reception at the Legion Hall, I saw

Sammy Kirkus again. This time he was riding his bike slowly along the sidewalk. Brent wasn't with him.

"Hello, Dog Breath," he said as he pedaled by me.

"Jerk," I yelled.

Sammy made a dumb face and shouted, "You look goofy."

Robyn hitched up her long dress and jogged toward the sidewalk. Sammy looked back at me and yapped about my "sissy-looking dress."

"Sammy!" Robyn shouted.

As he turned around to see who it was, Robyn lifted her arm. She aimed her hand directly at his open mouth. For a moment, I thought she was going to punch him in the face. But my best friend has more class than that. Her hand was full of birdseed. She dumped the whole handful into Sammy's mouth.

Sammy wobbled, swerved off the sidewalk and crashed into a large bush at the edge of the lawn. Robyn winked at me and then merged back into the thinning crowd.

A small group of remaining guests, Grandpa among them, decided to check out whoever was thrashing in the bush with their feet flailing in the air. I walked over and watched Grandpa help a spluttering Sammy to his feet. Sammy looked terribly embarrassed as he blew the birdseed out of his mouth.

"You all right, son?" Grandpa asked.

Sammy spat more birdseed onto the lawn, nodded once, jumped on his bike and rode off.

"Why would he eat birdseed?" Grandpa muttered.

"Probably because his doctor told him it was healthy," I said with a smile.

Grandpa chuckled. "Knowing doctors, that's probably true, Nic. And it's good to see you smile. You've been wearing a long face all day. I was starting to worry about you."

"I'm fine," I told him. "It's just such a busy day."

Grandpa gave me a quick hug. "I want you to be happy," he said. "You're my bestest granddaughter."

"I'm your only granddaughter."

"And my bestest," he repeated. "You know, I wish your grandmother had lived long enough to know you. She would have been really proud. You would have liked her, Nic."

"Grandpa, please don't smoke. And do all that other stuff the doctor wants. If you do that, I'll be happy."

"Now don't you start," he warned. "It's bad enough hearing it from your mother."

"It's just that I love you," I said. "And I want you to take care of yourself."

"I've done fine for the last sixty-one years and I'll be fine for the next sixty-one."

I knew why Mom nagged him. As she said, she didn't want to lose him. I knew how that felt.

3

The Question

We drove from the church to the Legion Hall. Robyn and I sat at the head table with the rest of the wedding party.

During the meal we had to jump to our feet whenever someone made a toast. And the guests kept clinking their spoons on their wine glasses. Every time they did that, Mr. Manning and Mom had to kiss. I wished they'd stop doing it. How many times did they have to see the newlyweds kiss? Surely, once was enough.

"This is going to be a boring party," Robyn said while we were waiting for dessert.

I pointed to the DJ setting up at the far end of the hall. "I don't know about that. There's going to be a dance."

"So what. There's absolutely nobody to dance

with," she grumbled. "How can we have fun when there are no boys?"

"There's my Aunt Alicia's kids. They're boys," I said. "You can dance with my cousins."

"Whoopee," she grumbled. "One is six and the other is eight."

"Arthur is almost nine."

"What's the difference? He's still a little kid. And who wants to dance with something called Arthur anyway?"

"You're being nasty," I said.

The waitress brought a piece of wedding cake and Robyn poked at it with her fork as if she was testing to see if it was real. "Sorry. But I'm mad. You'd think that in a crowd of a hundred and fifty people, there'd be a least one seventh or eighth grade boy. Oh well, at least we'll have fun at your pool party next week. We'll have to make sure we invite Brent."

"Yes, we will, won't we?" I agreed.

She winked at me. "You can show him around your farm."

For some reason, I felt embarrassed.

The dance started right after dinner. Of course, Mom and Mr. Manning were the first to dance.

"They look so good together," Robyn said.

"I suppose," I replied.

Robyn was right. They did look great together. I couldn't remember ever seeing Mom so happy. But I didn't like watching them. I wished I could make everything disappear.

"You ever think about who you'll marry?" Robyn asked.

"Are you kidding?"

"I think about it all the time," Robyn confessed. "Especially the wedding night."

"You've got a one track mind."

"You know that play, 'Romeo and Juliet'?" she asked. "You know how old Juliet is in that play?"

I shrugged. "Twenty-five?"

"Nope, she's thirteen."

"Thirteen," I said. "Get serious. She's not thirteen."

"She is too. Girls got married young in those days. If you were sixteen and not married, you were an old maid."

"I don't believe it."

"I read it in *Tattle Tale*. They had an article that said the real Romeo was a macaroni salesman and the real Juliet was an alien."

"What?"

"The article said they didn't have real proof, but that this teacher in Alaska had a dream about it being true."

"Huh?"

"Anyway, Tattle Tale told all about the play. It said Juliet is thirteen and Romeo is fifteen."

"I'm glad I wasn't around then," I told her.

"I don't think it would have been all that bad," said Robyn.

"Think about it, Robyn."

"Parts of it wouldn't be that bad?"

"I'm starting to worry about you."

"Then again, maybe you're right. Maybe it was the pits," she said. "Your parents decided who you were going to marry. I would probably have got stuck with some bozo like Sammy Kirkus."

"You guys would be a beautiful couple," I teased.

She replied by making a loud barfing noise. Several of the guests turned and stared.

Robyn wasn't fazed by the attention. "Another *Tattle Tale* story said it's fairly common for newlyweds not to do it on their wedding night. The article said they have such an exciting day, they're too tired to do it."

I stared at her. "It?"

"You know."

"Right. You know. *Tattle Tale* is full of all kinds of useful information."

"It sure is," she agreed.

"Excuse me, young ladies," Mr. Manning interrupted. "May I have this dance, Nicole?"

I tried to discourage him. "I'll stomp on your feet. I don't know how to dance if I have to hold on to somebody."

He arched one of his bushy eyebrows, the same way Mr. Spock does. "Then I'll teach you."

I guess Mr. Manning is a good dancer. I didn't have a clue what I was doing, but he led me in such a way that I didn't trip or step on his shoes. He smiled at me and I tried to smile back. I wasn't sure if it looked genuine or not. At one point, he planted a kiss on my forehead. I noticed Mom wearing a huge grin as she watched us.

By then, lots of other people were dancing. I saw Robyn go past, trying to keep her feet out of the way of her partner, my cousin Arthur. Arthur was jerking Robyn's arm up and down like a pump handle. When we passed again, Robyn gave me a look that said, Will this dance ever end? I also noticed Grandpa coming back from the washroom. That was the third time he'd gone since supper, no doubt sneaking cigarettes.

The music stopped, but Mr. Manning continued to hold my hand. "There's something I want to talk about, Nicole. Let's go outside for a walk."

"We shouldn't leave the party," I said. "You

shouldn't leave Mom. Besides, we're not exactly dressed for a walk."

"We'll be fine," he replied. "We'll just walk down the street and back. And it's your mother's idea. She says we have something to sort out."

I felt self-conscious strolling down Main Street dressed in my long bridesmaid dress holding hands with my old teacher who was wearing his best suit. A couple of times I tried to ease my hand free, but Mr. Manning held on.

Fortunately, all the stores were closed and nobody was around to see us. There wasn't even a crowd outside the Burger Baron. We talked about the weather and the wedding and how good the hay crop was going to be. None of this had to be *sorted out*.

When we reached the Safeway parking lot, we turned around and headed back to the Legion. I was really starting to wonder if Mr. Manning was ever going to get to the point.

He finally let go of my hand and shoved his hands into his jacket pockets. "Nicole," he began. "About the wedding . . . "

"Mom told you I was a little nervous about it, huh?" I volunteered.

"She mentioned your feelings," he said, "and I guess that's given me the courage to ask you an important question. I'm almost afraid to hear your answer."

Afraid to hear my answer? I thought.

"Two years ago, when you were in my class, you were a delightful student. You always seemed so happy. You enjoyed everything we did in school."

"It was a great year," I agreed.

"And even last year, you were definitely pleased whenever I came to visit your mother on the farm."

"You made Mom happy."

"But when I started dating your mom, that changed. You didn't seem all that happy to see me any more. And when we announced our engagement, you went out of your way to avoid me. You didn't even want to talk to me."

"I talked to you," I said in my own defense.

"Barely," he said. "You were just being polite."

I couldn't argue with that.

"And I've been a foolish person," he continued. "I'm a teacher and I should know better. I should have asked this question before. As I said, I didn't ask because I was afraid of your answer. But here it is, the first day of our new family, and considering what you told your Mom this afternoon, I have to know. Tell me the truth, Nicole, do you like me?"

"Of course I do."

A teenage couple came out of the movie theater.

They were all huggy, and laughed as they walked past us. They're probably laughing at our clothes, I thought.

"Are you happy about the marriage?" Mr. Manning asked.

"Not exactly," I told him. And then I tried to explain how I felt, the same way I'd done with Mom.

"I guess we both should have discussed our feelings earlier," he observed.

"I guess so, Mr. Man— Barry," I said. "You know, it's not just the changes I'm afraid of. It's more than that. But I don't know how to explain it."

He reached over and took my hand again. "I'm going to make you a promise. Although I know I'm never going to replace your father, I'm going to try to be the best stepdad a daughter could ask for."

Replace my father? My father was such a good dad that he died on me, I thought bitterly.

"And I promise I'm never going to be afraid to talk to you again," Mr. Manning went on, "and I want you to promise the same thing."

I made the promise even though I didn't want to. Talking to Mr. Manning wasn't making me feel any better. I wished he hadn't made his promise about being a good stepdad. It made me feel uncomfortable. And I felt even more uncomfortable because I didn't know why.

Mr. Manning slowed our pace as we got closer to the Legion Hall. "Your mom mentioned something about you and Robyn wanting to have a party next week."

"When have you guys had time to talk?" I said in surprise. "You've been eating and kissing all evening."

He smiled. "You'd be surprised how much you can say between kisses. Anyway, about the party, the answer is no."

"What?"

"Your mom's initial feelings were correct. It's not safe to have children out at the pool without an adult supervisor."

"Children!" I almost shouted the word. "I'm in junior high."

He ignored my objection. "And it's essential to have an adult supervisor at a mixed party."

I didn't know what to say. My jaws seemed locked in numb shock. Mr. Manning couldn't do this. He couldn't overrule Mom.

He seemed to sense my objection. "I've explained it to your mother. She understands now."

That made me angrier. He said it as if Mom had been stupid before, as if he had to show her just how stupid she was. I yanked my hand out of his. "Now let me get this straight —"

"Lower your voice, Nicole. We're talking, not arguing."

"Let me get this straight," I repeated just as loudly. "I can go swimming at the gravel pit, which is deep water, with a bunch of boys and, that's okay. But I can't have a few friends out to my pool to swim in shallow water. That's stupid, Mr. Manning."

"Your mom and I are responsible for what happens on the farm. If something went wrong, we'd be to blame."

I actually growled at that comment. "I lied before," I snapped. "I don't like you. I don't like you at all."

I twirled around and stomped, as hard as I could in my high-heeled shoes, up the sidewalk and back into the hall. Mr. Manning called my name a couple of times, but I ignored him.

I didn't know why I'd lied to him. I guess it was the anger talking. I did like him. I liked him an awful lot. But, and here's the weird part, telling him I disliked him made me feel good.

I was major confused, but for the first time all day, I felt good.

Maybe this is how people feel when they're crazy, I thought.

I expected a big scene from Mom when Mr. Manning told her how I'd behaved and what I'd said. But for some reason, he didn't tell her. He came back into the hall wearing a comfortable smile and went on celebrating as if our argument hadn't happened.

"That shows he's not really interested in me," I mumbled to myself. "And that's just fine with me, because I feel the same way about him."

✦ ✦ ✦

Before Mom and Mr. Manning left for their honeymoon, Mom took me aside. "You take good care of Grandpa tonight," she said. "He'll drop you and your bike off at Robyn's tomorrow before he drives back to the Hat."

"He doesn't have to do that. Robyn is going to pedal out and have lunch with me. We'll bike into town in the afternoon."

"All right. Take care of yourself, hon. I'm going to miss you."

I hugged her. "And you take care of yourself too. Don't do anything dangerous like deep-sea diving."

Mom laughed. "We're going to Banff."

"Don't climb any mountains then."

She laughed again. "Don't worry. It's long walks, good food and hot tubs all week." She watched a single tear roll out of my right eye. "Why are you crying?"

"I'm just happy for you," I lied.

"You should be happy for both of us," she said. "We have a whole family again."

"I am." Another lie.

"Are you disappointed we cancelled your party?" she went on.

"No." Lying was so easy.

Mr. Manning joined us. "We have to get moving," he said to Mom. "We have a three-hour drive."

Mom said goodbye with a long kiss. "Remember, we'll call you at Robyn's on Wednesday evening. And Mrs. Baker has the phone number of our hotel in case you need to reach us."

Mr. Manning said goodbye with another promise. "We'll talk as soon as I get back," he said.

"I didn't mean what I said outside," I told him.

He smiled a warm, gentle smile. "I know you didn't."

"What was that about?" Mom wondered.

"Nothing," Mr. Manning said as they left.

Why had I told him I didn't mean it, when I'd felt good telling him I disliked him?

Majorly confusing.

✦ ✦ ✦

The party continued for quite a while after they left. "We can start phoning kids tomorrow about the pool party," Robyn said at the end. "What day do you want to have it?"

"As soon as possible," I told her. "How about Monday afternoon?"

"Terrific," Robyn beamed. "Monday afternoon it is."

4

The Farm

Robyn biked out to my farm just before noon on Sunday morning.

By the time she arrived, I'd been up for hours. Even though I'd gone to bed really late because of the party, I'd had trouble falling asleep. And once I did fall asleep, I had trouble staying that way. My dreams woke me up several times.

They weren't nightmares, but they were definitely strange. In one, Dad and I were in the corral. The calves were sick with something that stopped them from eating, and we had to give them shots. I was struggling to get one skinny runt away from its mother when I looked up and saw Dad walking across the field toward the trees. I called to him and asked him where he was going, but he didn't turn around. He just kept walking, leaving me on my own. I yelled that I couldn't catch the calves by myself, that they'd all starve and die, but he vanished into the bush.

In another dream, I was back in fifth grade. The other kids were outside at recess, but for some reason I was doing a math test full of division questions and other stuff I couldn't understand. Suddenly Mom appeared at the door. "Nicole," she said. "I don't mean to interrupt your important test, but I thought I'd better let you know Barry and I are going on a little honeymoon. We may be back sometime. Then again, we may not. Take care of the cows and the bees and the chickens and don't have any parties with boys, and if we don't see you again, remember, we do love you and hope you have a good life."

Maybe this is how crazy people dream, I thought.

✦ ✦ ✦

Grandpa slept in, and he'd just finished brunch when Robyn arrived. "Well," he announced. "Now that you've got company, Nic, I'd better not dawdle. If I leave now, I still won't get back to the Hat much before dark."

After he'd gathered his bags, I walked him across the yard to his car.

"I wish you could stay longer," I told him. "I

hardly had a chance to visit with you."

"I've been here three days," Grandpa said. "That's long enough. Besides, I've got a golf game tomorrow."

We did the hug and kiss thing.

"Don't smoke, Grandpa."

"Don't start that again," he warned.

"Cut the fat off your meat."

"Just like your mother," he grumbled.

"Medicine Hat is so far away," I said. "I wish you lived in Picture Rapids. That way I could see you more often. Every time you say goodbye, I wonder when I'm going to see you again."

We hugged and kissed again. Then he got into his car and was gone.

"One minute he's here. Next minute he's gone," I said to myself.

"I'm hungry," Robyn declared when I returned to the house. "I'll have whatever smells good in here."

"I made Grandpa an omelet," I said. "I can make one for us too."

"What are you waiting for?"

Five minutes later, Robyn and I were eating one of my world-famous farm-fresh aero-omelets. Mr. Manning had taught me how to make them. He added a few drops of water to the bowl before cracking the eggs. "The water boils or something and makes lots of holes in the eggs. They're always fluffy," he'd told me.

"This omelet tastes terrific," Robyn said with a full mouth. "But how come it looks so funny? How come it's so yellow? It's almost orange. Eggs aren't supposed to be this color."

"You're just used to supermarket eggs. Those are laid by psycho chickens."

"Psycho chickens?"

"They spend their whole lives stuck in a little cage eating grain that goes by on a conveyor belt. Mom says it's really cruel to keep an animal locked in a tiny cage for its entire life. It makes them go crazy. They're so hyper that if there's a thunderstorm half of them have heart attacks and die."

I thought about Grandpa.

"No kidding," Robyn said.

"We feed our chickens grain, but they also free range," I explained. "They eat wild seeds and grass and bugs. That makes the yolks really dark."

"Bugs. Yuck."

"Our chickens are healthy. They sure taste a lot different than the ones at the Colonel."

"Taste different?"

I nodded. "Next time we kill one, I'll invite you out for a meal. Their meat is darker. That's because supermarket chickens don't get to use their muscles in the cages. White meat comes from flabby muscles."

"You kill your pet chickens?" Robyn asked the question as if I'd just confessed to murdering someone.

"They're not pets. They're farm animals."

"Still," she said. "They live with you. They're part of your family."

"They're farm animals," I repeated. "We're never cruel to them, but it's just a fact that none of the animals on this farm will die of old age."

She shivered. "I don't like to think about that. Let's talk about something else. Let's talk about the party. I managed to get in touch with Tanya and Cheryl this morning. They can come tomorrow afternoon. The rest of the kids are either away for the long weekend or at church."

"That's a start anyway."

"We'll try other people this afternoon," Robyn went on. "Especially the boys."

✦ ✦ ✦

Robyn followed me down the trail to the hay shed and corral. "That's a big cow in there," she said. "How come she's sitting in the muck all by herself?"

I smiled. "It's not a cow. If he was standing up, you'd be able to see it's our bull. And he's sitting in the mud because he's the laziest bull in the world."

"How many bulls do you have?" Robyn asked.

"Just one. One is all we need."

She seemed surprised to hear that. "So he's the husband of all your cows?"

I nodded.

"How come he's not out in the fields with them?" she wondered. "Shouldn't he be out there doing . . . you know."

"He had a hoof infection," I told Robyn. "The vet didn't want him tracking around the fields until it was all cleared up. And, for your info, most farmers want their calves born in the early spring. So he's probably already done *you know* for the year."

"Oh, he deserves a rest then," she said. "He sure looks fierce."

"He isn't." I laughed. "He's really mild-mannered. In fact, we call him Clark Kent because he's such a wimp."

We walked alongside the pasture toward the aspen-spruce forest which covers the back area of our farm.

"You haven't said how much you like my new belt," Robyn said. "My mom got it for me in Edmonton last week."

"It's a nice belt," I said.

"The little designs in the leather were made by

hand," she bragged. "The buckle is silver plated."

"It's a nice belt," I repeated.

"I look good in jeans, don't I? I mean, I have a nice shape for jeans, don't I?"

I smiled. "Whatever you say."

Robyn stopped and gently touched the top strand of the barbed wire fence that surrounds the pasture. "These little pointy things are sharp. I guess they stop the cattle from pushing on the fence, huh?"

"Yeah," I answered. "And the fact that it's an electric fence."

She jerked her hand away. "It is? I didn't feel anything."

"The top and bottom wire aren't electric, just the middle one. Hold onto it," I said.

"No way."

I did it myself. "It doesn't hurt. Honest."

Robyn cautiously copied me. She began to giggle. "It feels funny. It's like I'm buzzing. How does this stop the cows?"

"I'm not sure. Mr. Manning tried to explain it to me once, but I didn't really understand. I know if you have bare feet or if you touch the ground with your other hand while holding the wire, you get a jolt. And I know the fact that cattle have four legs means they get a real smack."

We continued to walk down the path until it led into the trees. "I come here a lot," I told her. Then I began to run. "Race you to the creek."

I ran, zigzagging between the trees and clumps of bushes, jumping over the deadfall.

"Hey," Robyn yelled. "Wait up."

I waited at the top of a small moss- and grass-covered rise until she caught up with me.

"The creek's down here," I said. "It's small, but I think it's beautiful."

"Maybe some of the boys at the party would like to come here for a walk. It's sort of romantic."

"Boys. Boys. Boys. Do you ever think of anything else?" I asked.

"Sure," she said. "I also think about boys."

We both laughed.

"I'm real glad we're best friends now," Robyn declared. "It's funny how we were in the same class three years in a row and didn't say much to each other. And then we got stuck as partners on that science project before Christmas, and we decided we liked each other."

"I always liked you," I said. "I just thought you were a little spacey."

"Spacey?"

"Yeah, you never took anything seriously. You still don't."

"Spacey?" she pondered. "That doesn't sound like a good thing to be."

"Flighty might be a better word."

"Flighty? That sounds even worse."

"I'm not insulting you," I pointed out. "It suits you. I wouldn't want you to act any other way."

"You want me to act spacey and flighty?"

I smiled. "I think you're fun to be with. You make me happy. Now if you'd only listen to me when I talked about serious stuff, you'd be perfect. Come on. Let's explore."

We walked a short way and Robyn stopped abruptly. "Hey, there aren't any bears in here, are there?"

"Probably not. I've only seen one bear on our farm. I think I was five years old. I was with my dad. When it saw us, it ran away. Mom did see some bear droppings this spring, but not a bear."

"Bear droppings?" said Robyn, sounding puzzled.

"Bear poop," I explained.

"Bears poop?"

"Of course they do. Everything does."

"Bear poop. Ewww."

"Anyway, I don't think there's any bears around," I said. "Not now anyway."

"What do you mean . . . not now? Did someone shoot them all?"

I couldn't help myself. Despite Robyn's anxiety, I had to laugh at her. "Nobody shot the bears. With all the noise we've been making, any sensible bear would have taken off by now. They don't want to mess with people. My mom says that if a bear sees you, it's long gone. If it hears you, it's long gone. If it smells you, it's long gone."

Robyn sniffed her armpits. "I sure hope I smell bad." Then she fearfully studied the bush for several moments, peering between the trees. "I have a funny feeling," she announced. "It's like I can feel a bear around here. I think I sense a bear."

I continued to laugh. "It's just your imagination, Robyn. There aren't any bears around. The creek is down here."

"All right, you're the farmer. You know about this stuff," Robyn said cautiously. "But let's make lots of noise. I don't think I smell bad enough." She belted out a few lines of an old Madonna song.

"You are one lousy singer," I said.

"I know," she agreed. "Maybe it'll scare away the bears."

We walked to the creek. It isn't all that wide, more or less a glorified ditch. It gurgled lazily between wide grassy banks.

I pushed through a small clump of willows and edged down the bank toward the piece of board I'd slung across the creek the year before.

"A bridge," Robyn said. "Good move."

We walked across the plank and sat down on the grassy slope. Clumps of marsh marigolds grew along the side of the creek.

"Sometimes I wish I lived in the country," Robyn told me. "Even if there are bears around. It's nice here. It may surprise you, but before we became friends, I'd never been on a farm."

"That certainly is a big surprise," I said sarcastically.

The sun was summer-warm, and I felt really peaceful. We lay quietly for a few minutes, soaking up the rays and listening to the birds singing in the trees. For the first time in days, thoughts about Mr. Manning and the marriage drifted away.

"What's that weird clucking noise?" Robyn asked.

"A squirrel. That's their noise. They chatter like that."

Robyn rolled onto her stomach. "Maybe it's calling for a mate. You want to go look for it?"

"They mate in the spring."

"Boring," she grumbled.

I closed my eyes. The sun made everything behind my eyelids look pink. Then little green dots started to dance into view.

"We've got to make a few more plans for the pool party," Robyn said. "We can ask everyone to bring snacks and sodas, but we're the hosts. We need to supply the hot dogs and marshmallows. I sure hope this weather holds. If it rains tomorrow, we'll have to have it Tuesday. Okay?"

"Okay."

"We'll set up your blaster on the deck so we can dance," Robyn said. "I'll bring my tapes and . . . AAARGGGHHH!"

"What?" I blurted. "What are you screaming at?"

She leaped to her feet. I quickly imitated her.

"Robyn," I shouted. "What's going on?"

"I saw something over there." She pointed to a clump of bushes further along the creek.

"What did you see?" I asked. "For heaven's sake, you scared me to death."

"I'm not sure. It was big. No, it was huge. Maybe a bear. Maybe a deaf bear that didn't hear all the noise we were making. Maybe a deaf bear who can't smell. Let's get out of here. I saw something. Honest."

A branch snapped and we both gasped. Robyn grabbed my arm, and made a little whimper. A patch of willows along the creek began shaking and rustling. Something was after us.

5

Yucky

Robyn and I went from fear to panic at the same time. In a uncoordinated mess of arms and legs, we charged for the plank and collided, almost knocking each other into the water.

"Ooof," I protested.

"Oooh," Robyn grunted.

I pushed my friend in front of me, and we scrambled across in single file. Suddenly, Robyn stopped and I plowed into her back.

"Ooof," Robyn protested.

"Oooh," I grunted.

Robyn twisted around, dropped quickly to one knee and started tugging violently at the board. "Quick," she hollered. "Help me wreck the bridge."

"Don't be stupid," I yelled. "The creek's small enough to jump across."

"Good thought," Robyn agreed. "Let's boogie."

I was ready to crank into a first class sprint when a large brown head appeared in the willows, a large brown head with cow horns.

"It's a wild moose," Robyn screamed as she ran up the bank. "It's a wild moose with rabies."

"Wait," I called. I recognized the white half-moon on the animal's face. "It's not a moose. It's one of our cows."

Robyn stopped halfway up the slope and quickly turned to study the animal. "One of your cows? What's it doing here?"

The cow stepped from the trees and, after looking in our direction briefly, started drinking from the creek.

"I didn't think cows wandered around in the woods," Robyn said. "I thought they hung around in fields."

"It's our missing heifer," I explained. "We got her last fall. When the guys were putting up the electric fence last year, they left the pasture gate open. Some of the cattle got loose. We caught them all except her. We didn't see her all winter, so Mom thought she must have found her way to another farm or been rustled, or starved."

Robyn came slowly down the slope and stood beside me. "Is it safe?" she whispered.

"Yeah," I assured her. "I wonder where she's been."

"So it's a wild cow?"

"Sort of."

"I'm glad it's not a bear."

"Me too," I confessed. "I was really scared."

"I wasn't," Robyn declared. "I was just being cautious."

"Right, I could tell. You were full of caution."

She smiled wanly. "It's better to be safe than eaten."

The heifer stopped drinking and looked at us. Then she turned and walked slowly into the bushes beside the creek.

"Hey," Robyn yelled, "what's that yucky thing hanging out its rear end? It looks like a giant bubble-gum bubble."

"Holy!" I gasped. "She's going to have a calf. That's the waterbag. Wherever she's been, there was a bull around. Come on. We have to follow her. Don't make too much noise. We don't want her to take off."

"What? Why do you have to follow her?" said Robyn.

"Because we don't want to lose her now that we've found her, and because I'll have to check the calf when it's born. Come on."

We crossed the creek again and walked as quietly as we could along the bank.

I held out my arm to stop Robyn. "Look. She's lying down. If we don't go any closer, she'll stay there. She's probably in labor."

We backed off a little way and waited. After a few minutes the cow's side started heaving.

"She's having contractions," I whispered.

Quickly, two front feet and part of the head of the calf appeared inside the waterbag.

"Wow," Robyn whispered. "I've never seen a cow have a baby before. It's gross."

The cow strained again, and a bit more of the head and feet appeared. We waited. So did the cow. The contractions started again, but the calf didn't come out any further. Then the contractions stopped altogether.

"Uh-oh," I said.

"What?"

"Something's wrong. I think it's stuck."

"Stuck?"

I nodded. "It should be all out by now."

"What next?"

"We'll give her another minute to see what happens. If she can't deliver the calf herself, we'll have to help."

"Help? How can we help deliver a calf?"

"Keep your voice down," I warned.

"How-can-we-help-a-pregnant-cow?" Robyn whispered the sentence as if it was one long word.

"We're going to have to get hold of the calf's front feet and pull it out. I've seen the vet do it."

"Why don't you call the vet then?" Robyn asked.

"Because before he has time to get here, that calf is going to be dead."

"Wow. Won't the cow attack us if we try to help? Don't cows bite?"

"The worst thing that will happen is she'll stand up and run away. Then there'll be nothing we can do."

"I'm real nervous, Nicole."

"Me too."

"You're nervous too? Great. Terrific. Good. That makes me feel a whole lot better."

We waited a while longer. The cow strained a few more times, but the calf didn't move out any farther.

I sighed. "We have to do it. Move quietly. Let's not scare her." I walked slowly towards the cow. She gave a loud, long moo. Behind me, I heard Robyn stifle a gasp. The cow didn't move.

"We're not going to hurt your calf," I cooed in my sweetest voice. "We're going to help."

The cow mooed again.

"It's me," I told it. "Remember me? I'm Nicole. I

used to feed you your chop. I like calves. I'm just going to help you."

The cow shuddered and I froze. Then it raised its head and studied me.

"I'm going to help the calf," I said again.

The cow seemed to understand because she slowly lowered her head to the ground and relaxed.

I knelt down behind her and Robyn crouched beside me. She looked at the calf's head and feet, still inside the waterbag. "Yuck! What do we do first?" she asked.

I pressed my index fingers into the waterbag and ripped it. Clear fluid sloshed onto the ground. I tore the bag away from the calf's nose.

Robyn made a gagging noise.

The calf's tongue was hanging out of its mouth. I ripped the bag away from its feet.

"Okay," I said. "When the cow pushes again, help me pull on the calf's feet."

"They're all slimy. I'll get my hands yucky. I hate having yucky hands."

"You can wash them later. Don't be such a wimp, Robyn. This is important."

The cow strained again, and I grabbed the calf's legs. "Come on. Pull."

Robyn gingerly touched the calf's legs beside my hands.

"Hold on tighter," I ordered.

She closed her eyes and grimaced as she grabbed the legs. We pulled.

"That's good," I said.

The cow strained once more.

"Pull harder," I coached.

The calf came out a tiny bit more. But only a bit. We weren't getting anywhere.

"My hands keep slipping," Robyn whined. "They're all yucky."

"Give me your belt," I said. "We'll wrap it around its legs to get a better grip."

"Use your own belt."

"If you opened your eyes, you'd see I don't have one. I'm wearing my shorts."

"But it'll get yucky stuff on it."

"Robyn!" I whispered through my teeth.

"Do I have to?"

"Give it to me."

Robyn wiped her hands on her jeans, removed her belt and handed it to me. I buckled it around the calf's legs.

This has to work, I thought. This just has to work.

I handed the free end of the belt back to Robyn. "This time you pull on the belt, and I'll tug on the calf's legs. Ready?"

The cow strained again and we pulled. “It’s coming,” I said. “Harder.”

Robyn grunted.

The calf slipped out so quickly that Robyn and I were thrown off balance. We sprawled backward, landing on our rear ends with a thud.

“Ooof,” I protested.

“Oooh,” Robyn grunted.

Another gush of clear fluid followed the calf.

“Grossening!” Robyn shrieked as it oozed under her backside.

“Lower your voice. You’ll scare the cow.”

“Scare the cow?” she protested as she stood up and cautiously examined the back of her jeans. “Scare the cow? My bum is covered in . . . in . . . baby cow juice and you’re telling me I’ll scare the stupid cow?”

I eased myself up and pointed at the calf. “Sssh. Look.”

The calf shook its head to clear its nostrils. Then its whole body shuddered as it started breathing. It gave a short moo, more like a bleat. I grabbed a handful of grass and wiped the gunk off its nostrils.

“It’s going to be fine,” I said triumphantly.

Robyn was silent for a few seconds as she watched the skinny, wet calf take its first breath. “We did that, didn’t we? We borned a baby cow. That sounds stupid. A baby cow was borned by us. We helped born it. Whatever, we did it."

"He's a bull," I pointed out. "Or can't you tell the difference?"

She slapped my shoulder. "Of course I can."

The calf was light brown with white feet. He had the same white half-moon in the center of his face as his mother had.

"He's awful wet," Robyn said.

"His mother will clean him up and he'll dry. Let's move back."

As I said that, the cow suddenly lurched to her feet. Robyn didn't need a second invitation to scamper out of the way. I unbuckled her belt from the calf and joined her.

The cow made a low motherly moo as she started licking her calf. "That's sort of cute," Robyn said.

"We'll just wait and see if he gets to his feet and starts feeding, okay?"

"I'm sorry I was so . . . you know, so slow to help," Robyn said."

"You did what had to be done. I couldn't have done it without you. You were great."

"I was, wasn't I? But you were so much better. You were in control. You were really terrific."

We looked at each other and smiled. Then we slapped sticky hands like football lineman do after they sack the quarterback.

The cow continued to lick her calf roughl,y and I couldn't help but feel proud of what we'd done. We held our breath as the calf made his first attempt to get to his feet.

"It's standing up," Robyn said.

Not for long. He fell flat on his face.

"Ooof," Robyn protested.

"Oooh," I grunted.

The calf tried a few more times. It flopped over each time.

"Is this normal?" Robyn queried. "It's not sick, is it?"

"It's normal," I said. "He'll stand up eventually."

Finally the spindly, shaky legs supported him and the calf stood for a few seconds. Unfortunately, his mother licked him at that point, and he toppled over.

Robyn groaned. "How come she did that? Why is she so mean?"

"That's normal too. He's trying again."

The calf staggered to his feet and managed to stay up. He fumbled alongside his mother in search of his first meal. It took him a long time to find the udder, but at last we heard the sucking noises which meant everything was the way it was supposed to be.

"Everything's cool," I said. "That's all we can do for now. Let's go back to the house."

"Good idea," Robyn said. "I've got to get out of these clothes and take a shower. You'll have to wash everything I'm wearing. I feel so . . . "

"Yucky," I finished for her.

"Exactly."

I handed Robyn's belt to her. As we crossed the creek, we washed our hands in the water and Robyn rinsed the belt.

"There. It's wet but clean." Then she glanced at the cow again. "Nicole, are you just going to leave the cow and calf here? Aren't you going to try to get them back with the other cattle?"

"They won't move for awhile," I told her as we threaded our way back through the trees. "And I've got a plan to trick her back to the corral."

"Are you going to name the calf?" Robyn asked.

"If you want. I sometimes give them names."

"Let's call him Sammy," Robyn suggested. "He was so stupid that he couldn't even be born the right way."

"No," I disagreed. "That wasn't his fault. Besides he's too cute."

"Call him Brent then," Robyn suggested. "That's a cute name."

"All right," I said. "We'll name him Brent."

✦ ✦ ✦

I lent Robyn my robe and threw her clothes in the washing machine. She took a shower while I waited on the deck, wondering what Mom and Mr. Manning were doing that very minute.

"I suppose I should make more of an effort to call him Barry," I said to myself. "I can't go on thinking of him as Mr. Manning. That's too formal. He's Barry, my stepdad."

Then again, I didn't make him fall in love with Mom. I didn't make them get married. He was my stepdad, but I didn't have any choice in the matter. So he was really still my old fifth grade teacher, Mr. Manning. And that's all he'd ever be.

"Thinking of him as Mr. Manning is just fine," I said.

"Who were you talking to?" asked Robyn when she joined me.

"Myself."

She twirled a finger around in front of her forehead and crossed her eyes.

"I'm not crazy," I protested. "It helps me think."

"I feel much better," she announced. "Even though I don't look it. Your robe doesn't look as good as my jeans. Lucky there are no boys out here."

"You looked real good in your jeans with a wet butt," I pointed out.

“Speaking of clothes, did I tell you what I’m going to wear for the party?”

“Your bathing suit?” I guessed.

“Nope.” She shook her head. “I’m going to borrow Barbara’s bikini.”

“Your sister will let you?”

“She won’t know about it. I’ll just take it.”

“And when she finds out, you’ll be toast,” I warned.

“It’s really skimpy,” Robyn bragged. “I’ll look so great in it.”

“If it’s really skimpy, it’ll fall off,” I said. “You have nothing to keep it up.”

Robyn glowered at me and puffed out her chest. “You’re just jealous.”

“Right,” I said.

“Speaking of bikinis,” Robyn said, “this reminds me of an article from *Tattle Tale*. The headline was *School of Fish Eats Woman’s Bikini.*”

“Give me a break,” I said.

“Honest. It said these hungry fish ate the swimsuit right off her body while she was swimming in the ocean. They liked whatever the bikini was made of, so they ate it.”

I started laughing.

“She had to run up on the beach naked when she couldn’t stand the cold anymore,” Robyn went on.

"Hundreds of people cheered."

"The reporters for *Tattle Tale* sure have great imaginations."

"I believe it," Robyn noted as she leaned over to study the water in my pool.

"You're not looking for fish, are you?"

She blushed and began to laugh too. We had a chuckle-fit that lasted for a couple of minutes. By the time we stopped my stomach hurt and I had trouble catching my breath.

"Thanks for the laugh," I said between wheezes. "I'm going to clean up now. Why don't you get on the phone and try to get more kids for the party?"

"It sure is great of your mom to let us have one," Robyn said. "I don't think my parents would ever let me have boys over if they weren't there."

And for the first time since I'd decided to have the party, I felt a twinge of guilt. Then I recalled Mr. Manning's lecture and his firm no.

I hope you get real mad at me when you find out, Mr. Manning, I thought. I hope it makes you hate me.

6

A Boyfriend Boyfriend?

Although we managed to invite a few more people to the party, nobody answered at Sammy's house. That meant we didn't invite Brent.

"Don't look so disappointed," Robyn said. "We'll try Sammy from my place this evening."

Before biking into town to spend the night at Robyn's, we walked down to the corral. I unhooked a stainless steel bucket from the wall of the hay shed and filled it from the chop bin.

"What's that?" Robyn asked.

"Cow food," I told her.

"I thought they ate grass."

"This is called chop. It's chopped up oats and barley. We use it in the winter and spring. It adds stuff that may be missing in the hay. I'm going out to give it to the new mother. You want to come?"

She declined. “All the way out there? I’m too tired from walking and phoning. I only have enough strength to pedal home. I’ll wait in your deck chair.”

The cow and Brent the calf were still by the creek. I gently banged the bucket with a stick as I approached, then dumped the chop in a pile in front of the mother.

Cautiously, the cow investigated the mound of oats and barley with her snout. Obviously delighted with what she found, she mooed and started eating.

“Eat up,” I said to the cow. “And tomorrow maybe I can trick you back into the corral.”

✦ ✦ ✦

We had a roast beef supper with Robyn’s parents and her older sister, Barbara. Robyn didn’t eat much meat.

“I’m not that hungry,” she said. “I keep thinking about the animals on Nicole’s farm.”

Dishes all stacked in the dishwasher, Robyn went to the family room to try and reach Sammy so we could invite Brent. I decided to take a walk to the school, three houses away.

“Mom and I usually go and check the cattle after supper,” I explained to Robyn’s father as he wiped the kitchen counter. “Taking a walk is a habit. I’ll only be a little while.”

A school is a very different place in the summer.

It seems so empty. There's nothing on the windows. The playground is clean, no chip bags or chocolate bar wrappers blowing around, no forgotten jackets at the ball diamond.

I walked around the back and peered through the windows of my sixth grade classroom. The bulletin boards were brown and bare. The desks were stacked up in one corner. It was like the class I'd belonged to just four days ago didn't exist any more.

Then I realized that, of course, it didn't. This wasn't even my school. Next September, I'd be in Picture Rapids Junior High.

Just like my dad, I thought. One day he was part of us, the next day he was history.

I'll never forget the sound Mom made when the police officer told her that Dad's truck had skidded on the icy road and flipped over. It was a sound so sad and so full of pain, more a wail than a cry. I still shiver when I think of it.

I'd been playing with my Barbies on the living room carpet when it happened. For a moment I froze, watching the cop help Mom to a chair. Even though I was only eight, I knew Dad was gone forever. I cried for two days. My Aunt Alicia and Mom's friends tried to comfort me, but there was no way to stop the tears.

After the funeral, I tried to make deals with God. If only he'd make Dad alive again, I'd promise to clean my room every day. I'd eat my vegetables. I'd become a missionary. Anything. Just make Dad alive.

I stopped mourning two weeks after the funeral. Mrs. Stevens, our neighbor, was visiting, and I overheard Mom tell her about the police report of Dad's accident.

"They did a blood check on Steve," Mom said. "There was alcohol in his blood. Rachel at the Legion said he'd dropped by the lounge for a couple of hours after he'd picked up the antibiotics from the vet. She said he only had a few beers, but the police said he was going too fast. They said he wouldn't have skidded if he'd been going slower. They also think he might have survived if he'd been wearing his seat belt."

I stopped mourning and got really mad at Dad. How could he do something so stupid? How could he drink and drive? How could he speed on icy roads? Why wasn't he wearing his seat belt? Didn't he care about himself — or us?

Remembering, I wiped the mist out of my eyes, wandered to the playground and sat down on one of the swings. I hadn't been on a swing for a year. For some reason, it was sort of an unofficial rule at our school that sixth graders were too old and too cool for the swings.

"I fell off you in first grade," I said to the swing. "Did I ever bump my head."

I pumped my legs to get the swing going, and pretty soon I flew level with the bar. It felt great to have the wind whipping my hair and whistling in my ears.

"Whoo!" I called out loud.

And then I saw somebody out of the corner of my eye — somebody leaning against the teeter-totter, watching me. When I recognized who it was, I nearly died of embarrassment.

It was Brent.

I let my feet drag to slow me down and hoped my face wasn't completely beet-colored.

He walked toward me. "Hi," he said. "It's Nicole, right?"

I nodded. "I don't usually ride the swing," I muttered as I slowed to a stop. "I was just goofing around. I don't really like it."

He sat on the swing next to me and looked at me with those incredible brown eyes. "You seemed like you were having fun."

"Well, in a goofy sort of way," I said.

"You looked real neat," he went on. "The way your hair flew out behind you one way and then covered your face the other way looked . . . neat."

"It did?"

"Yeah." He pumped his legs to get his swing moving. "Bet I can go higher than you," he challenged.

"No way," I said.

A minute later we were both so high the swings snapped as we came back down. Brent laughed up a storm, having a great time, so I laughed too.

Just like with Robyn earlier, I laughed so hard I ran out of breath and had to stop.

"A-1," he said after I'd recovered. "That sure was great. You're lots of fun, Nicole. I'm glad we moved to Picture Rapids. I've only been here two days, but I already like it better than Toronto."

"You're glad you left Toronto to come to Picture Rapids, Alberta?" Was he for real?

"Sure. I'm going to miss my mom and the Blue Jays, but nothing else. Everything is so uncrowded here. Everyone is friendly. Like you."

Miss his mom? I thought. I was curious about why his mother wasn't in Alberta with him, but I didn't ask.

"My mother says Picture Rapids is too friendly," I said. "Everybody knows everybody else's business. How come you moved here anyway? I don't think I've ever heard of anybody else moving here from Toronto."

"My dad got tired of his job," Brent explained. "He was a salesman for a hardware supply company. The traffic drove him crazy, so he bought a Home Hardware franchise, 'as far away from Toronto as a body can get.' That's how he put it, anyway. So here we are."

I smiled. "I never thought Picture Rapids was as far away from Toronto as a body could get. It doesn't sound like much of a compliment."

"You're really pretty when you do that," Brent said. "You should smile more often."

For a few seconds, I didn't have a clue what to say next. Finally, I told him the truth. "No boy has ever said I'm pretty before. It sounds weird. Nice, but weird."

He seemed a little embarrassed. "I'm sorry. I'm doing it, aren't I? It's because of my counselor."

"Counselor?"

"You know, a psychologist. A person who helps you out when you're having problems."

"Oh." I was curious, but it didn't seem polite to ask him what his problems were.

"You want to hear about it?" he volunteered.

"I guess so," I told him. "If you want to tell me, that is."

"It's no big deal, really. My folks got divorced a few years ago. When my dad remarried last year, I had a few problems. Nothing serious. I goofed around at school. And I was rude to Mary, my stepmom. So they sent me to a counselor who taught me to say what was on my mind. I have trouble remembering I'm only supposed to do that with my family. Sorry again."

"It's okay," I said. "It was different, but it was also nice."

"Sammy told me your mom married your old fifth grade teacher," Brent went on. "That must be kind of weird, huh?"

"Kind of," I agreed. "It's kind of neat, too. But there's part of me that doesn't like the idea at all."

"Just like me. My counselor told me most kids get confused when one of their parents gets married again."

I wanted to tell him about my doubts. I felt that, unlike Robyn, he would listen to me. But I stifled the impulse. I hardly knew him. Besides, he was a boy. You don't discuss personal stuff with a boy.

Then again, wasn't he telling me personal things? You don't tell a complete stranger you went to a counselor, do you?

"Do you have a boyfriend?" Brent wanted to know.

"I've got lots of friends who are boys."

"No, I mean a boyfriend boyfriend? You going with anybody?"

"Going with anybody? Of course not. I only just finished sixth grade."

"Some of the sixth grade kids at my old school were going out with each other. I guess that's just in Toronto."

"What's going out with someone mean at your old school?" I asked.

"It means that you hang around together. Go to the show, grab a burger, stuff like that."

"I thought it meant like . . . going steady."

He shook his head. "Sort of like a best friend, but it's a girl. I mean, it's a boy to you."

"Then I'm definitely not going with anybody."

He smiled. "Good. What are you doing tomorrow, then? Maybe we can do something together."

"I'm having a party tomorrow afternoon," I told him. "A pool party at my farm. You're invited, if you want to come."

"Great." He grinned. "How do I get there?"

"It's only a couple of kilometers out of town. Do you have a bike?"

He nodded.

"Then you can ride out with Sammy. Robyn's probably already invited him by now. He knows where I live."

“Super, I can hardly wait. I have to run now. I’m already late. It’s my dad’s turn to cook tonight — supper will be on the table by now. See you tomorrow.”

“See you,” I replied as he jogged across the playground.

“I like him,” I said to myself. “I really like him.”

✦ ✦ ✦

While Robyn and her family slept, I sat propped up on the pillows of the guest bed, staring into the semi-darkness, trying to figure out why things were happening the way they were.

Robyn had managed to get in touch with most of the kids in our class, including Sammy. I was hoping Sammy was still away. Now that I’d invited Brent we didn’t need birdseed breath. There was going to be quite a crowd at the party. Mom definitely wouldn’t approve when she found out. Not approve? She’d flip out. She’d told me no.

Mr. Manning would freak too. Good. That’s what I wanted. I wanted him to think I was untrustworthy and disobedient and not a nice person. I wanted him to dislike me so much he’d stay out of my way.

But why did I want that? It wouldn’t make everything the way it used to be. Mr. Manning would still be living with us. He’d still be Mom’s husband, kissing her good-bye as he went off to face the fifth graders every morning.

I sighed out loud and thought about the party some more.

Mom had left me in charge of chickens and checking the cattle. Helping to birth the calf proved I was responsible. Having this pool party was just another responsible thing to do. If I could do all that other stuff, I could have a quiet, friendly party where everyone came out, had a swim and went back home. No big deal. Why couldn't Mom and Mr. Manning see that?

Why didn't I care what they thought?

No, that was wrong. I did care. Mom would be so disappointed. So would Mr. Manning. He'd be shocked. I'd never be able to face him.

Good. That was my plan, wasn't it? I'd be happy. But I'd be unhappy at the same time.

Confusing.

✦ ✦ ✦

It was well past two o'clock before I fell asleep. I didn't feel any better when I woke up. Robyn noticed my sour mood as we ate breakfast by ourselves.

"What's up, Nicole?" she asked.

So I confessed. I explained how Mr. Manning and Mom had told me not to have the party. "Tell me that it's okay," I said as I poured another bowl of cereal. "Tell me doing this behind my mom's back is okay."

Robyn's reaction didn't surprise me. "Wow," she said. "I never thought you'd do anything like that. I thought I was the only one who'd do something . . . something so sneaky. But don't worry about it, Nicole. I'd do the same thing. It's not as if you're doing something really bad, is it?"

"That depends on how you look at it."

"Lighten up," she coaxed. "Everything will be fine. Think of how much fun you'll have with Brent there. Besides, there's over twenty kids coming. You can't cancel now."

No, but I felt that twinge of guilt again. This time it wouldn't go away.

7

A Stinky Situation

On the way out to the farm, we stopped at the supermarket for hot dogs, marshmallows and assorted bags of crunchy junk food. With a fair amount of coaxing, easing and shoving, we managed to squeeze everything into our backpacks.

"It's a miracle it all fits," Robyn observed.

Maybe miracle was the wrong word. When we dumped the stuff onto my kitchen counter, the chips, tacos and pretzels were definitely the worse for wear.

"What a mess," I said. "Everything is all bashed up."

"So what? It'll still taste the same," Robyn reasoned.

I ripped open a bag of sour cream and onion

chips and peeked inside. "You want to eat some potato flakes?"

"Nobody will notice. Besides, the others will bring stuff," she said as she pulled two long silver threads out of her pack.

"What's the silver string for?" I asked.

"It's not string. It's Barbara's bikini. I took it out of her dresser this morning."

I examined the almost non-existent pieces of cloth. "There's nothing to it. It won't cover anything."

"It stretches," she told me.

"Your dad lets Barbara wear this?"

"She can only use it to sun in the back yard. My aunt was in Europe last year and bought one each for Mom and Barbara. It was supposed to be a joke, but Barbara wears hers anyway."

I stared at it.

"Don't look so worried, Nicole. It stretches."

"I'll take your word for it," I said. "But it sure will have to stretch an awful lot."

"The boys will like it."

"I am definitely worried about you."

"You're interested in boys too," she countered. "Do you realize how many times you've mentioned Brent's name since you invited him to the party?"

"A couple?" I said defensively.

"Eighteen times," she corrected. "I've been counting. So don't give me a hard time about boys."

"Speaking of Brent," I said. "Let's go check on mom and calf and see if we can get them back to the corral."

I grabbed the stainless steel bucket from the hay shed. This time I only half filled it with chop.

We walked to the creek, crossed the plank, but couldn't see the cow or her calf anywhere.

"This will bring her," I said. I rattled the metal pail of chop with a stick and, sure enough, mother and baby appeared ten seconds later.

"I've got something for you," I said softly. "You remember the yummies from yesterday?"

I left the bucket on the ground and the cow rammed her nose into it. She quickly scarfed down the food.

"She sure is hungry," Robyn said.

"It's the chop. Cows love it. They'll eat the stuff until they're bloated."

"Now that I'm close to her again, I know why I was afraid yesterday. Cows are scary," Robyn noted. "I mean they're so big. And those horns look real sharp."

We backed up a little and watched the cow eat while the calf sniffed at some willow leaves.

"I love that little white half-moon on his head. Brent sure is cute," I said.

"Both Brents are cute," Robyn pointed out. "Hey, I just remembered something else from *Tattle Tale*. They had this story once about a farmer who loved his cow so much he married it and . . ."

"Let me guess," I interrupted. "They had a child, and it was half cow, half person."

"Almost," Robyn said. "Actually, they had twins. A boy who was perfectly normal except that he only ate grass, and a girl who was just like a cow except she liked playing with dolls."

"I believe that," I told her.

Robyn smiled. "Me too."

When the cow finished, she looked up and mooed loudly. Robyn moved further back. I walked slowly toward the cow. "That's all there is, mom. See?"

I picked up the pail and turned it upside down. "You want some more, then you follow me back to the corral."

The cow lowered her head and bellowed.

"What's it doing?" Robyn shrieked.

"She's telling me she's angry because there's no more chop."

"She looks like she's going to charge," Robyn said. "Like at a bull fight."

"She won't. Come back!" I shouted as Robyn

headed for the creek. "We have to go the other way to the pasture."

The cow bellowed again, a long, angry moo. "No way, Nicole," I heard Robyn yell as she crossed the plank. "I'll go back this way. I'll meet you at the house."

I had to admit the cow did look a bit wild and, if you weren't used to cattle, kind of frightening.

"It's all right," I assured Robyn. "She's not dangerous. This is normal behavior for a cow."

Obviously, Robyn didn't believe me. She was scrambling up the rise on the other side of the creek.

"Hey, don't be a wim—"

"Eeeeeggghhh," Robyn screamed. "Oh no! Ooooogggghhh! Help me, Nicole. Please, help me. Uuuuggghhh."

A shiver shot through my insides. What was wrong? Why was she screaming like that?

"Help me, Nicole!"

I dropped the bucket and ran toward her. I was so hyped I didn't use the plank — I jumped across instead.

"What's wrong?" I called. "Are you all right? What on earth is wrong?"

Just as I caught a glimpse of a small, black and white shape disappearing into the tall grass, I was hit by an overpowering stench.

Skunk.

"Help me," Robyn howled. "Oh yuck, help me."

I came closer and stopped. Robyn, tensed up, was trying not to inhale too deeply. In self defense, I began to breathe through my mouth. I don't think I've ever smelled anything so awful.

I knew skunk spray could be dangerous if it hit you in the eyes. "Did it get your eyes?" I asked.

"No, my jeans and T-shirt," she told me. "But my eyes are watering. And I can't breathe through my nose. What am I going to do?"

"Look Robyn, I'm not going to come any closer. You smell too bad."

"Thanks a lot," she whimpered.

"We'll go back to the house and we'll clean you up. Okay?"

She nodded miserably.

"Try to look on the bright side," I said as I skirted around her, keeping my distance, and clambered up the slope.

"The bright side?" she moaned.

"At least it'll keep the bears away," I told her.

She didn't smile at my feeble joke. "Follow me, but don't get too close," I instructed.

I looked back to see Robyn trailing along behind me, her face scrunched up into a wrinkled mess. She was moving stiffly, her arms held away from her body. I turned away so she wouldn't see the smile that crept across my face. Although I'd never tell her, she sure looked funny.

At the house, I said, "You can't go inside smelling like that. We'll never get rid of the reek. Take off your clothes and I'll hose you down first."

"Take off my clothes? Here? In front of your house? In the middle of the yard?"

"Nobody can see you from the road," I said.

"It's not that. What if some of the boys come for the party?"

I glanced at my watch. "It's not even lunch time. Nobody is coming until later."

"Somebody might come early. I'm not going to take the chance."

I ended up spraying Robyn in her clothes. The cold water only made her feel more miserable.

"It's freezing," she shrieked. "Stop! Let me go into the house and take a shower."

"Take off your clothes just inside the front door," I ordered. "Then throw them out."

"Aren't you going to wash them?"

"Robyn, smell them. They're history."

She started to cry. I wanted to go over and give her a hug, but I couldn't. Despite the wash down, she continued to radiate a strong stench.

Robyn went into the house. Half a minute

later, the offensive clothes sailed out the door. I picked them up with our garden rake and heaved them into the rusty oil barrel we use to burn our garbage.

Robyn was so long in the shower, I checked to see if she was okay. "Are you still in there?" I called.

"Yeah," she called back. "I don't think this smell will ever come off."

I went to my room and took a T-shirt, shorts and underwear from my dresser. When I opened the bathroom door, clouds of steam poured out. "Here's some clean clothes."

We sat on the deck while Robyn let her hair dry in the sun. "Do I smell okay now?" she asked. "I think I still smell the stink."

"Me too," I said.

"Oh, no. What am I going to do? It's almost time for the party."

"Maybe you don't smell any more," I suggested. "Maybe we're just so full of skunk we're still smelling it."

"I hope so," Robyn said. "I'd die if Kyle thought I smelled bad."

"Kyle?" I said, puzzled. "Why Kyle?"

She covered her face with her hands for a moment. Then she peeked between her fingers. "I didn't mean to say that."

"Kyle? The same person you tried to glue to his desk last fall?"

"The very same," she admitted. "Now that you know, I might as well be honest. For the last few weeks I've been thinking how good-looking he is."

"I guess. But he's so small," I said. "He only comes up to your shoulders. And his hair is longer than yours."

"He told me he's growing it so he can be in a heavy metal band when he's older."

I couldn't picture Kyle in leather and Spandex.

"And so what if he's short?" Robyn went on. "Haven't you noticed most of the guys our age are shorter than us? Just because Brent is tall . . ."

"Don't get upset. I like Kyle," I said. "Why didn't you tell me before?"

"You would have teased me."

"Of course I would," I grinned. "That's what friends are for."

"Don't tell anyone, okay?"

I crossed my heart and held up my hand. "Only if you promise not to say anything about Brent."

"It's a deal," she agreed as she inhaled deeply. "Do you really think I still smell?"

"I told you, I'm not sure."

"Isn't there anything I can do to be positive I don't smell?"

"I heard that if you take a bath in tomato juice it gets rid of it."

"That sounds disgusting," Robyn said. "But I'll do it. How much tomato juice do you have?"

"None. I hate the stuff. But I've still got the perfume my grandpa gave me for Christmas last year. It's in my top drawer. Try putting some on. At least, that'll cover it."

"Thanks. First, I'm going to take another shower."

While she did that, I returned to the creek, held my nose as I ran through the skunky area, and picked up the chop bucket. As I hoped, the cow quickly appeared, definitely interested in more oats and barley. She followed me as I threaded my way along the trail behind our cleared fields. I unlatched the back gate to the pasture and the cow, with her calf at her heels, obediently wandered in as if she'd never been away.

Five minutes later, secured in the corral, mother greedily ate more chop as baby nursed.

"You'll be safe here," I said. "The other cattle are in the back pasture. You only have to share with Clark Kent. That bull's too timid to bother you. He's only interested in cows in heat."

Clark Kent sniffed the cow for a few seconds before losing interest.

Back at the deck, I found Robyn dabbing her eyes with a Kleenex. I choked back my breath. "Gosh," I gasped.

She wiped away the tears. "I think I used a little too much. It's making my eyes water, just like the skunk."

"It smells as bad as the skunk," I added. "How much perfume did you use?"

"Half the bottle."

"Half the bottle? You're only supposed to use a little. A drop on each cheek."

"I thought if a little is good, then a lot is better."

I shook my head. "Wrong move."

"Where do I find clean towels? I'm going to take another shower."

I vacuumed the pool and set TV trays on the deck for the snacks and drinks.

Robyn emerged from her third shower, dressed in my T-shirt and shorts, carrying my blaster and a handful of tapes. She put them on the picnic table.

"How do I smell now?" she wanted to know. "I didn't put on as much perfume this time."

"You smell much better," I told her.

Actually, I thought she still smelled like skunk. It was as if the odor wasn't completely gone, just mixed up with the perfume, creating a new skunky-sweet aroma. But then again, my nose had been bombarded with some pretty gruesome smells in the last hour. Maybe I was just imagining things.

"I thought you were going to wear Barbara's bikini."

"I'm saving it for later," she said. "I want to make a big entrance."

"I'm sure you will. My turn in the bathroom now."

I grabbed a quick shower. Quick, because there was no hot water left. It started out lukewarm and passed rapidly through cool to cold.

When I went back outside, a car was pulling into our driveway. Monica and Cheryl were inside, waving. A few minutes later, Tanya, Jill and Ramona showed up on their bikes. Kathy's mom drove up next. She had Kathy and Kathy's friend Magda with her.

As the girls got out of the car, Kathy's mom looked suspiciously around my yard, probably looking for an adult in charge. But when she saw me watching her, she flashed a big smile, waved and drove away.

My stomach tightened up. What was I doing? Kathy's mother worked in Safeway. The next time Mom went shopping, she'd talk to her about my party. Mom would come home mad. Mr. Manning would be angry. I'd be grounded until the next century.

Why was I doing this? This wasn't like me. I'd never done anything to hurt Mom before.

But I didn't want to hurt Mom. It was Mr. Manning I was trying to upset. But why? I did like Mr. Manning. He was kind. He loved Mom.

And I could tell he loved me.

He'd never said it aloud. But I could tell by the little things he did, the way he was so interested in how I was doing in sixth grade, the way he offered to take me bowling or skating, the way he held my hand when he walked with me.

So why was I deliberately trying to upset him?

You still have time to call it off, I thought.

8

Sammy's Surprise

I couldn't just cancel the party. Six people had already arrived. More would be here at any moment. I couldn't disappoint them. Then again, I was going to disappoint Mom and Mr. Manning.

"Where are the boys?" Kathy asked. "I want to meet the new guy you told me about on the phone, Robyn. Where's Bart?"

"Brent," Robyn corrected. "And he'll be here. Lots of boys are coming."

I had to think of that too. If I called off the party, I wouldn't get to see Brent. I wanted to talk to him some more. I wanted to show him around my farm.

Magda handed me a plastic bag full of pop cans and snacks. When I carried them into the kitchen, the framed picture of Mom and Mr. Manning caught my eye. It had been taken the winter before when we'd gone skiing in Jasper. They looked so happy, locked arm in arm, grinning at the camera. I remembered how they'd joked with me when the lens cover stuck and I fumbled with it.

"You're such a klutz, Nicole," Mom teased.

"But we love you anyway," Mr. Manning added.

For some reason their eyes seemed to be staring at me, as if they could see what I was doing. I removed the photo from the wall and placed it face down on the counter.

Robyn and a couple of the girls came into the house. "You can change down the hall," Robyn was telling them. "The first door on the right is Nicole's room."

She walked over to me and I noticed the weird skunky-sweet smell again. I thought maybe I should say something.

"You don't look all that excited," Robyn noted. "You thinking about what you're going to say to Brent?"

I shook my head. "I'm just wondering what I'm going to say to Mom and Mr. Manning. I'm not sure the party is a good idea any more."

"Worry about that later," Robyn coached. "This is the time for fun. Look." She pointed out the window. "Here come the boys."

A gang of guys on BMX and mountain bikes were pedaling down my drive.

Robyn ran outside and I peered through the window. I picked out Kyle and Sammy Kirkus in the crowd. And Brent. He saw me looking at him and waved. I waved back.

I went into the bathroom to make sure I looked the best I could. As I brushed my hair, I noted how much I looked like Mom. It was eerie in a way, almost like she was on the other side of the mirror staring at me.

"All right," I said to myself. "Sure you're feeling a little guilty, but don't get weird."

On my way out of the bathroom, I met Allan Yeung in the hall.

"Hi, Nicole," he said. "I really like your pool. It's going to be a great day for a swim. I brought my snorkel and flippers."

"Have fun," I said. "You can get changed in the guest room on the left."

"I don't mean to be rude or nothing," Allan went on. "But something smells funny out there. Sort of like a skunk, but it isn't. Maybe you should check around."

"I'll do that," I said.

I have to talk to Robyn, I thought.

The boys had brought their own pop and snacks,

and I was kept busy putting the stuff in the refrigerator. It seemed like we had enough for an army.

By the time I got outside the party was well under way. The deck was crowded with kids and the music had been cranked up. Several people were already in the pool.

The conversation on the deck was a loud buzz, but I did hear someone say, "You guys smell a skunk or something?"

One of the boys jumped off the edge of the pool and splashed a lot of kids, causing a symphony of hollers and shrieks.

"No jumping off the edge," I shouted. "It's dangerous."

Everyone ignored me. Everyone except Sammy Kirkus. He stood beside me, dressed in neon green swim shorts. "It's dangerous? Boy, Nicole, you've only been a teacher's daughter for a few days and already you're giving out rules."

"Bug off."

"Is that any way to treat a guest?" he asked. "I'm gracing your stupid party with my presence."

"Bug off, please."

"What a dope," he chuckled as he walked away.

"I'm thirsty," someone yelled. "Where's the pop?

"Inside," I said. "I'll get it."

Robyn was sitting with a small group of kids. I tapped her on the shoulder. "Come help me get the drinks."

She groaned.

"You're co-host, remember?" I said. "Besides I have to talk to you about something."

She stood up and reluctantly followed me inside. "You're a real grouch. What's wrong? Hasn't Brent spoken to you?"

I pulled cans of pop from the fridge and placed them on a tray. "I told you I'm worried about what my mom and Mr. Manning will —"

Robyn didn't let me finish. "Nicole, there's nothing you can do about it now. Just relax and enjoy yourself."

With those great words of wisdom, she took the trayful of drinks outside.

"And you still smell like a skunk," I said to an empty kitchen.

A minute later, I brought out my own tray of pop and chips. The party was even noisier than before.

"Hello, Nicole," somebody shouted over the hubbub.

I turned around and discovered Brent smiling at me. He pointed to his ears and mouthed the words, "It's so loud."

Robyn pressed her face in front of mine. "We need more pop."

"You go get it," I said.

"What?"

"You go get it," I shouted.

"I can't. I'm talking to Kyle."

"I don't mind helping, Nicole," Brent volunteered.

I stared daggers at Robyn, but she didn't notice. She was too busy gawking at Kyle.

Brent and I went into the house. "You have a nice place," he said. "It's not like I thought it would be. Not your house, I mean. Alberta. Somehow I thought Alberta would be flatter. You know, prairies. No trees. And I thought it would be more western. I thought everybody would look like a cowboy and ride horses around. Everybody looks the same as in Ontario."

"They do have a rodeo in Picture Rapids in August," I said.

He seemed excited to hear that. "Great."

"And I've got a pair of cowboy boots," I bragged. "Somewhere."

Brent dumped some chips in a bowl as I grabbed another six pack of Coke. "Do you have a horse?" he asked.

"I used to a couple of years ago, but Mom sold it.

She said it didn't do anything, and it cost us a fortune in feed and vet bills. She bought me a trail bike instead."

"A trail bike? Decent. Can I ride it sometime?"

"Sure," I said. "It's only a 50 cc., and I haven't used it this year because it needs a new plug and stuff. Why don't you come out again soon and help me tune it up?"

"You bet," he agreed. "I'd really like that. And I'd like to see all of your place. Will you show me around later?"

"I'll take you down to the creek," I said. "It's my favorite spot on the whole farm." I thought about what Robyn had said about it being a romantic place.

"Your mom must be really different," Brent observed. "I mean to let you have this party when there's nobody home."

"Yeah, well . . . "

"Hey, everybody!" somebody outside shouted. "Come and see what Sammy's doing."

I glanced out the window and saw half the kids jogging toward the corral.

"This doesn't look good," I said. "Let's go."

Brent and I followed the kids down the trail to the corral. By the time we arrived, they were all leaning on the wooden gate watching the activity inside. I heard lots of laughter and someone say, "Isn't he brave?"

I peered around the crowd and over the fence. "I don't believe it," I said. "Of all the dumb things."

Sammy was standing in the middle of the corral, grinning stupidly at everyone as he petted our bull.

"Should he be doing that?" Brent asked.

"Get out of there," I yelled.

I wasn't worried about Sammy's safety. "We call our bull Clark Kent because he's so tame," I told Brent. "He likes it when someone pays attention to him. But Sammy doesn't know that. Why would he do something so dumb?"

"That bull looks really big," someone said. "I'd never be brave enough to go near it."

"You want me to get him out, Nicole?" Brent asked.

"I'll do it," I said. I walked over to the barbed wire fence. "Get out of there, Sammy. The cattle are off limits."

"You going to make me?"

"You want me to put a fresh cow pie in your shorts?" I answered.

His grin vanished. "You wouldn't do that."

"You've got five seconds," I warned.

"You wouldn't do that," he repeated.

"Four seconds."

"You're bluffing."

"You want to find out? Three seconds."

"I'm not afraid of you."

"*Fresh* cow pie," I threatened. "Still steaming. Two seconds."

"There's no way . . ."

"One second."

My expression convinced him. He stopped petting the bull and headed for the fence. I lifted the top strand of wire so he could climb through.

But Clark Kent wasn't prepared to give up a good scratch so easily. He hustled behind Sammy. Sammy turned to pet him one last time. Unfortunately, he decided to touch the bull at the same moment he placed his hand on the middle string of barb wire . . . the electrified string.

Just like Robyn had earlier, Sammy only felt a slight vibration. But the bull, standing on four legs, got a healthy zap. He bellowed, twisted and leaped sideways, snorting and tossing his head, eyes wide open, showing lots of white.

Sammy screamed and dove madly through the fence, snagging his swim shorts. There was a loud tearing noise and I noticed a large piece of ragged, neon material hanging behind Sammy like a tail. His audience, at first startled into silence by the reaction of the bull, began to hoot and holler.

"Moon river . . . " somebody started singing. That made everybody, including me, laugh. Sammy scrambled to his feet, fumbling to cover the rip.

"Serves you right," I said.

He didn't say anything, just walked away up the trail backwards as the crowd broke into applause.

The party moved back to the deck. Soon people were swimming and dancing again.

"Would you like to dance, Nicole?" Brent asked.

"I'm not that good," I said.

"Me neither."

Brent watched me with a big smile on his face as we danced. That made me feel more clumsy than usual.

Sammy returned to the party dressed in his cut-offs. A few of the kids razzed him, but they stopped pretty quickly when Robyn bounced out the front door, wearing Barbara's bikini. She was right. It did stretch. But not that much.

Robyn walked along the deck to the accompaniment of whistles from the boys. It was obvious she was enjoying being the center of attention. She had a big grin on her face as she jumped off the edge of the deck into the pool.

"Ooo," Brent moaned.

"You think she looks good, huh?"

"I didn't mean that," he said. "It's that smell. Sort of like skunk."

We danced through another song and Brent said, "I'm going in to get changed. I want to go for a swim. You want to get wet?"

"Maybe later," I told him.

Somebody had spread a towel on the deck, and I sat down on it. I closed my eyes and tried to convince myself I was having a good time. In a way, I was. Talking to Brent and dancing was fun. Sammy's accident was a hoot. But I kept hearing my mother's voice in my head. "Nicole, how could you?"

"Let's eat," one of the boys yelled. "I'm hungry."

"Me too," someone else called.

Everyone poured out of the pool at the same time. I got up quickly because they dripped cold water on me.

I heard Robyn giving instructions. "There's a brick barbecue and wood over there. Get a fire going, you guys. We'll roast some hot dogs. I'll get the stuff out of the refrigerator. Give me a hand, Nicole."

Great, I thought. Back to work.

Robyn and I went into the kitchen. "This is a great party," she said. "I'm really making an impression on Kyle. How are you doing with Brent? He really likes you. I can tell. I mean he really, really likes you. If I were you, I'd —"

She stopped because Brent had finished changing and was walking down the hall. "Hi, Brent," she said. "We were just talking about you."

He sniffed a couple of times, scrunched up his nose and then shrugged. I had to tell Robyn about her unusual aroma.

"I'll see you outside," Brent said. "I still want to have that tour of your farm."

"He's such a hunk," Robyn said after he'd left. "Are you going to take him to the creek?"

"Maybe," I said. She gave me a friendly elbow in the ribs.

"Robyn, there's something you should know —"

"Oh, no," Robyn exclaimed and pointed out the window. "Tell me later. There's Kyle talking to Kathy. I have to put a stop to that." She dashed outside.

"You still smell like a skunk," I said to the empty kitchen.

9

Just Gnarly

After the food, the party settled down a little. Some people went back into the pool. A few others danced, but they turned the blaster down because some of us were sitting talking in small groups. I sat in a group of two — me and Brent, under the pine tree on our lawn.

We talked about our sixth grade classes, then about Toronto and Picture Rapids, Alberta and Ontario, Sammy's accident, and finally about our families.

Brent told me about his mother. " . . . and so after the divorce my mom went back to university in Kingston. That's three hours from Toronto, too far for me to visit her every week." He was silent for a moment. "It felt like she'd left me as well as Dad. I knew it was logical for me to stay with Dad, and I knew Mom had to go to Kingston to get the courses she wanted. It all made sense, but underneath it still felt like she'd turned her back on me."

Another silence.

"Where is she now?" I said at last.

"She's still in Kingston. I used to see her about once a month. Like I said yesterday, I'm going to miss her."

I twirled a blade of grass between my fingers. "This may sound sort of crazy, but I felt the same way about my dad. When he died, I was majorly upset, but at the same time I felt angry, like he'd died on purpose. I was really mad at him for dying on us. That's weird, huh?"

He shrugged. "I don't know. What you went through is a lot different from me."

"I've never told anybody that before," I went on. "About being angry at Dad. Not even Robyn."

"How about your mom?"

"Are you kidding? She'd think I was crazy."

He flashed his cute, dimpled smile. "Maybe. But my counselor would tell you to say it anyway."

I leaned back against the tree and returned his smile. "You know, I've never, ever spoken to anybody like I'm talking to you. Never. And it's so strange." I held up three fingers. "I've known you this many days, and here we are discussing our feelings about our families."

"You're easy to talk to."

"And you're a boy."

He laughed. "Thanks for sorting that out for me."

I slapped his shoulder. "I just meant I never thought I'd ever tell a boy how I felt."

We watched a pair of bold magpies skirt the deck and try to steal chips from the bowls. Sammy, sunning on a deck chair, tried to peg one of them with half a hot dog. He missed and the bird flew away, squawking in protest.

"Can I ask you a personal question?" I said. "Yesterday, when you told me you were having trouble at school and you had to see the counselor, was it because of your angry feelings about your mom?"

He shook his head. "No. My school problems began when Dad told me he was going to marry Mary. I mean, I liked Mary a lot. Still, I got upset because I thought they'd get married and in a couple of years they'd split up, and I'd have to go through a divorce all over again. I didn't want to lose Mary the same way I'd lost my mom."

As soon as he finished talking, something clicked in my mind. It was like a light had been turned on. I could see something, even though I wasn't sure what I was looking at.

"What's wrong, Nicole?" Brent asked. "You look worried."

"No," I told him. "I was just thinking about what you said. Can I ask you another personal question? What did your counselor say to make you feel better?"

"That bit I just told you — about worrying Dad and Mary would split up? It was my counselor who pointed that out to me. I didn't really know what was bugging me before that. And then she helped me see that was stupid. Worrying about it, I mean. They might break up, they might not. Either way, I couldn't do anything about it. She helped me see I could enjoy Mary and Dad today and let tomorrow be tomorrow."

"Wow," I said.

"It sounds simple, but it didn't make sense right away," he continued. "It took a few visits before I could really do it. And I'm not sure . . ."

"Wow," I repeated. "Wow, wow, wow."

"What's that mean?"

"I'm not sure. But it has something to do with the way I feel about my grandfather. And maybe Barry. Brent, will you help me tell everyone the party is over?"

"What? The party is over? Why?"

"Maybe I'll be able to tell you later. Right now, I

just want everybody to go home. I think I understand why I'm doing this."

"Doing what? Sending everybody home?"

I flashed a big smile. "No, having the party."

"Huh?"

"It's got something to do with what you just said. Will you help me send everybody home?"

He hesitated, confused by my crazy logic. At last, he said, "It's your party. You can do what you like."

I glanced over at Robyn. She and Kyle were sitting in their own group of two. She'd be upset, but so what? She was my best friend. It was her duty to understand why I was ending the party — even though she wouldn't understand.

Heck, I didn't understand it completely myself.

As Brent and I stood up, someone in the pool splashed Sammy. Sammy went strange. I guess he was still embarrassed about the accident at the fence, because he screamed, "I'm not going to take that." Then he jumped off the deck and sprinted into our tool shed.

"Get out of there," I yelled.

He dashed out with two empty honey pails.

"Put those back, Sammy."

He ignored me. Quickly, he filled the buckets from the garden hose and charged back to the deck.

I tried to stop him, but he dodged around me and headed for the person in the pool.

I remember what happened next as if it were slow motion. I grabbed for him at the same moment he tripped on a towel. The honey pails flew from his hands and the water whooshed out of the buckets — all over the dancers and sunbathers lying on the deck.

Before you could say "water fight," everyone got up and headed for the pool.

"Hey, you guys, knock it off," I shouted.

No one listened. They were in the middle of World War III, using the drink tumblers and honey buckets to attack each other with pool water.

I saw a laughing Robyn, her hair plastered to her head, dump water on Kyle. He pushed her into the pool for revenge.

"Stop it," I ordered. "The party is over."

It was like whispering into a hurricane. Nobody could hear me.

"Look at that," Brent shouted into my ear. "Look at what's happening down by the corral."

I twisted around and saw Allan running up the trail. He was carrying one of our steel chop pails from the hay shed.

"Oh, no," I mumbled.

Allan looked scared. No, he looked terrified. And

it was obvious why. The corral gate was open and he was being chased by a jogging cow with a half-moon on her face.

I figured out what must have happened. When Sammy had gone in to pet the bull, he must have entered through the corral gate. He got out of the corral through the fence. That meant the gate was left unlocked.

Allan must have been down by the hay shed when the water fight broke out. He saw the excitement on the deck and decided to join the action with a major weapon, a chop bucket. The cow heard him rattle the bucket, figured it was chow time and pushed the gate open.

"Drop the pail," I yelled to Allan.

He charged up the steps onto the deck and screamed, "Mad bull!"

Slowly, shriek by shriek, chuckle by chuckle, squeal by squeal, the noise of the water fight quietened to a buzz, then a murmur, then a silence.

One by one, everyone noticed the lumbering cow.

"The cow is going to run onto the deck, Nicole," Brent said. "How can we stop it?"

The kids cleared the deck in a hurry. With a chorus of hollers, they jumped over the top rail onto the lawn or dived into the pool.

I ran at the cow and waved my arms to try to

drive her off. "Get out of here, cow," I yelled. "Go away."

But I wasn't far enough in front to make her turn around. She continued to lumber forward. I turned toward the pool. "Watch out!"

The people in the pool splashed to the far end. The cow thundered up the two steps onto the deck.

She's going to stop, I thought. She has to stop. She's not going to jump in the pool.

SPPPLLLAAASSSHHH!

"She jumped in the pool," I said aloud.

The animal mooed angrily and waded for the far end of the pool toward the kids. They screamed again and scrambled over the sides. The pool cleared as fast as the deck.

"Don't panic," I called. "Keep quiet. Don't scare her."

"I guess this doesn't happen often, huh?" I heard Brent say behind my back.

To make matters worse, the cow's calf arrived. It stood at the edge of the lawn, away from the crowd, and bawled.

"Shut up, Brent," I shouted. "Stop that. Don't get your mother more upset."

"Shut up?" said Brent, sounding injured. "Why did you say that? And my mother lives in Kingston, remember?"

"Not you," I said. "The calf. Brent the calf."

"Brent the calf?"

"He's named after you."

"You named a cow after me?"

"He's a bull."

"Oh," Brent said.

"I don't have time to explain now. There's a cow in my swimming pool."

The cow reached the end of the pool as the last of the kids scrambled out. She made a huge leap, trying to clear the edge. She almost made it. Unfortunately, her rear feet and a large part of her weight came down on the edge rail. She kicked her legs and stumbled over.

She stood near the pool, mooing to her calf. The little guy ran after her, and the two of them trotted back down the trail toward the corral. As they disappeared, I noticed something waving from the cow's horn.

"I'll go close the gate," Brent said as he followed them. "Okay?"

"Please," I said as I stepped onto the deck. Robyn suddenly ran past me, dripping water, her arms across her chest like she was really cold. She disappeared into the house.

I glanced at the pool and groaned.

Where the cow had landed on the rail, there was

a huge V-shaped dent. The rail and the metal side were badly buckled.

The kids gathered around me. They seemed to be in a state of shock.

"Holy," someone said. "Look at the pool."

"I'm real sorry, Nicole," Allan mumbled.

"I thought that bull was going to attack me," Kyle said.

"It wasn't a bull, it was a cow," someone told him. "Bulls don't have udders. That thing had an udder."

"What an incredible party, Nicole," Sammy said. "That was terrific. That was just gnarly. Awesome. Everybody will talk about your party for years."

"Everybody will remember your moon landing, Sammy," someone hollered. A couple of kids hooted their agreement.

I stared at the damaged pool as my insides fell into a lump. Of all the things that could happen, this had to be close to the worst. The pool was wrecked. How could I explain this to Mom and Barry?

"I don't feel like partying any more," one of the girls said.

"Aw, come on," Sammy said. "Things are only just warming up."

"Your mom is going to kill you," Allan said. "I'm real sorry."

And with that, the party was over. Everyone picked up their towels. Some went in to change or to call for a ride. Others just drifted off. A few people came up to me and mumbled things like, "Thanks for the party, Nicole. Sorry about the pool."

I just nodded numbly.

10

Boom. Boom.

Sammy was the last to leave. "Look, Nicole, I'd check under the deck if I were you. Maybe something died under there. I smelled something strange all afternoon. Sort of like skunky perfume," were his parting words.

Then there was nobody left but Brent and me. I leaned against the deck rail and stared at the pool. Robyn appeared beside me and put a hand on my shoulder. She was dressed in my shorts and T-shirt again.

"Don't worry," she said.

Brent joined us. "They're back in the corral. The cow looks okay. I watched it for awhile. It's eating hay, and the calf is nursing. Your bull is just sitting. The gate was open so I closed it. Oh, yeah, there's something silver hanging off the cow's horn."

"I know what it is," Robyn said.

"Look at my pool," I whispered.

"I'll ask my dad if he'll fix it," Brent said. "I'm sure he'll do it. He's pretty good at stuff like that."

"What a mess," I moaned.

"I'm in a big mess too," Robyn said softly. "When I go home I'm going to get destroyed."

"You? Why? Your mom won't give you heck about my pool."

"I'm not so sure about that," she disagreed. "But it's not Mom I'm worried about. It's Barbara."

"What are you talking about?" I asked.

"The bikini. That cow ran off with Barbara's bikini top."

"What?" I asked. "How?"

"I don't know. When the cow jumped into the pool, I did so much flapping that the top slipped off. I covered up and climbed out of the pool. Next thing I see is the top caught on the horn. It was so embarrassing. I'm lucky everybody was watching the cow. If anybody had seen me, I'd never have been able to show my face at school in September."

Robyn's problem seemed too trivial to worry about.

But Brent disagreed. "Let's go get it," he suggested to me. "It'll help take your mind off the pool."

✦ ✦ ✦

We slipped through the gate into the corral. The cow regarded us with her usual bovine stare.

"Barbara's bikini top isn't hanging on the horn," Robyn observed.

"It was there before," Brent assured her. "It must have fallen off."

"Yeah," Robyn said. "With my luck it's probably in the middle of a cow pie."

"Look around," Brent said. "It can't be far away."

"What's that?" Robyn exclaimed. "What's Brent eating?"

"I'm not eating anything," Brent replied.

"Not you." Robyn pointed at the calf. "That Brent."

"There it is," I said. "Brent is eating Barbara's bikini top."

Brent the person laughed and Robyn cried in frustration.

"Go slowly," I said.

We crept slowly forward, but even our cautious approach was too much for Brent the calf. He whipped his head around and ran away, the bikini top still trailing from his mouth.

"Drop that bikini you stupid, dumb, fathead calf!" Robyn yelled.

Her outburst startled the cow. She mooed and

stomped over to protect her son. Luckily, it scared the calf too.

He dropped the top and ran toward his mother.

Gingerly, I picked it up. Barbara's skimpy bikini top was transformed into a thin silver piece of string covered in cattle spit.

"Here." I offered it to Robyn.

"I'm not going to touch it," she said. "It's covered in yucky cow slime."

"Yucky calf spit," I corrected.

"What am I going to do?" she moaned.

"You'll have to tell Barbara what happened," I said. "At least you don't have to explain a wrecked pool."

"Do you smell something?" Brent asked. "I think there must be a skunk nearby. All afternoon, I've smelled this weird skunky smell."

"That's not a skunk," I told him. "You've just been smelling Robyn."

Robyn's eyes bulged open and her chin dropped. "It's me?" she gasped. "It's me? You mean I still smell? I thought it was my imagination. Why didn't you tell me?"

"I tried to," I explained. "A couple of times, but you were interested in other stuff."

"You mean I stunk all through the party?"

"I don't think anybody knew it was you," I said.

She dropped to her knees in the corral muck and buried her face in her hands. "Arrgghh," she wailed. "I'm going to be the first person to ever die of embarrassment. Kyle thinks I smell like a skunk."

✦ ✦ ✦

Two days later, Robyn and I were sitting on deck chairs, watching Brent and his dad studying the damaged pool. As Brent promised, his dad offered to fix the dent. We'd drained the water on Tuesday. Today, Mr. McGregor was going to work on it.

Brent looked up and smiled at me. I returned it.

"That's so cute," Robyn said.

"Don't give me a hard time," I warned. "I've heard you on the phone all week. You've said some pretty mushy things to Kyle."

"That's just for something to do," she defended. "You know I'm grounded in the evenings for two weeks for taking Barbara's bikini."

Brent's father shook the dented metal. It made a boinging sound.

"'Course, two weeks isn't that bad," Robyn reasoned. "And Barbara is so mad, she said she'll never speak to me again. So everything worked out for the best when you think about it."

"I wonder what my mom will do to me when she finds out about the party and the pool?"

"Maybe Mr. McGregor will fix it so well your

mom won't know it got wrecked."

"Everyone in Picture Rapids knows about my swimming cow by now," I pointed out. "Even if Brent's dad fixes the pool, Mom will hear what happened."

"Maybe not."

"Robyn, I'd tell her. I couldn't keep it a secret."

"Why don't we make a huge Welcome Home sign to string across the driveway?" Robyn suggested. "That way your mom will be happy when she sees the sign and won't be nearly so mad when she sees the pool."

I couldn't get up any enthusiasm to make the sign. It seemed too phony. "You know, Robyn, there's a side of you that's dishonest."

"I'm just creative," she said. Then she took a long sniff along each arm. "I'm sure glad I don't smell any more. And I'm sure glad nobody but you and Brent knew it was me who smelled so bad. If anybody knew it was me, I would have . . . "

" . . . died," I finished. Then I called to Brent and his father. "Can I get you something? A Coke? Some lemonade?"

"In a little while," Mr. McGregor answered.

"You know, Nicole," Robyn went on, "we could turn this into a money-making opportunity."

"Huh?"

"What happened here on Monday was sort of different, right?" she said. "I mean it's not every day somebody has a cow in their pool."

"You can say that again."

"I think it's different enough to have someone write a story about it. Like someone from *Tattle Tale.*"

"From *Tattle Tale?*"

"It's just the type of story they'd love. We could make the front page."

"Right next to the picture of the Titanic survivor they found on the iceberg? Get real."

"I'm serious," she insisted. "There's an ad in every issue that says they'll pay money for unusual stories. Can't you just see the headline? *Crazy Cow Causes Chaos.*"

"That's stupid."

"But they might pay," Robyn said greedily. "We'll be famous. People all over the country will read about us."

"That's the last thing I want," I said. "That is a definite no. And I mean it."

"Where's your sense of adventure?" she coaxed. "Maybe I'll just go ahead and do it by myself and get all the money."

"You do that and I'll call *Tattle Tale* with my own story," I threatened. "I can picture the headline now.

Amazing Skunk Girl Stinks Out Party."

Robyn bit her bottom lip as she thought about my comment. "You're right," she said. "Calling *Tattle Tale* about the cow is a stupid idea."

Brent's dad walked back to his car and returned with a large hammer in his hand. He bashed the outside of the pool.

Boom. Boom.

The noise was deafening. The pool acted like a giant drum.

Boom. Boom.

Robyn and I cupped our hands over our ears. Mr. McGregor hammered a couple more times, stopped to inspect his work for a moment, then hammered again.

It was during one of the breaks in the hammering that I thought I heard someone call my name. I turned around.

Mom and Barry were stepping onto the deck, frowning.

Boom. Boom.

Mom yelled over the noise, "What's going on? What happened to the pool? Who's that man? Who is that boy?"

Boom. Boom.

"A cow jumped into it," I yelled back. "How come you're back so early?"

Boom. Boom.

"What did you say happened to the pool?" Mom hollered.

Boom. Boom.

"A cow," I hollered back.

Mr. McGregor stopped for a moment.

"A cow jumped into it," I repeated. "The man is Mr. McGregor. He's from Toronto, but now he owns the Home Hardware. That's his son, Brent. He's in seventh grade. They're new to Picture Rapids. How come you're home so early?"

"It's been raining for the past two days," Barry said.

"And Barry told me about your argument outside the Legion Hall on Saturday night, Mom added. "We decided the way we left you wasn't right. We wanted to come home and straighten things out."

"I'm glad to see you." It was the truth.

"You did say a cow jumped into the pool?" Mom asked.

"It jumped off the deck," I said.

Boom. Boom.

Mom tried to say something but the pounding made it impossible. So she marched up to Brent's father instead. They talked for a few seconds and shook hands. Then Mom shook hands with Brent.

Mr. McGregor climbed out of the pool, introduced himself to Barry and went to his car again. This time he returned with a small propane welder. He eased back into the empty pool while Mom and Brent joined us on the deck.

Mom said, "Mr. McGregor thinks the damage won't be too hard to fix, but I'd like to know exactly how it happened. How on earth did a cow get into the swimming pool?"

Robyn and Brent stood close beside me to give me support as I told the tale.

It seemed like an awfully long explanation. I explained about the calf being born, Robyn and the skunk, the party, Sammy and the bull, Allan and the chop bucket, the cow in the pool, and Robyn's bikini top.

Mom kept a stern expression on her face. She concentrated on what I was saying. On the other hand, to my surprise, Barry smiled. His smile got wider and wider as I detailed each incident. By the time I finished, he was grinning.

Then it was Robyn's turn to surprise me. "It wasn't Nicole's fault," she said. "It was mine. I suggested the party. I pushed her into having it."

"Then I'm disappointed in you too, Robyn." Mom said. "But Nicole had the final responsibility. And she knew that I had said no."

“Nicole tried to fix things, Mrs. Peters,” Brent told Mom. “Just before the cow jumped into the pool, she asked me to help her tell the kids the party was over. I think she was feeling bad she was doing it behind your back.”

“That’s not all true, Brent,” I said. “It was something else too.”

Mom studied me for a few moments with a look of complete disappointment on her face. I wished I could shrink and ooze between the two-by-fours of the deck. “I’m not happy about what I just heard,” she said grimly.

And then Barry laughed. I saw Mom dig him in the ribs with her elbow to tell him to be serious. But I also noticed little wrinkles form around her mouth as she too tried not to laugh.

“Oh, Nicole.” She gave me a big hug. “What am I going to do with you? It’s a good thing I don’t go on a honeymoon more often.”

11

We Love You, Nicole

Brent's father put Robyn's bike in the back of his van and they drove back to town just before dinner. Our pool looked almost normal again and Mr. MacGregor said he'd reattach the lining the next day.

Mom suggested we have a barbecue for supper.

"And just because I laughed doesn't mean that I'm not as upset as your mother," Barry lectured me from across the picnic table. "To say I'm extremely disappointed is an understatement of how I feel." Then his stern teacher-face dissolved into a web of middle-age smile lines. "But every time I picture a cow in the swimming pool and Sammy with half a pair of shorts, I can't help myself. It's just so funny."

Mom sat down beside Barry and put the cooked hamburgers on the table. "Well, I don't find it humorous. Somebody could have been hurt."

"I'm sorry." I apologized for the sixtieth time. "I know it was dumb of me. That's why I did it. I wanted you to be angry at me for being so stupid."

Barry took a hamburger and began to load it with canned pineapple, peaches and fruit cocktail. "I know we should have talked about your feelings before the wedding. I could sense you were uncomfortable about things. I blame myself for not sitting down and discussing it then. But you should have known us better, Nicole. You didn't have to make your Mom and me angry to get our attention."

Mom pointed at Barry's hamburger. "I don't know how you can eat that mess."

"You haven't lived if you haven't eaten a fruity burger," Barry responded. "Nicole thinks they're great too."

"No I don't." I reached for a hamburger and poured a dollop of ketchup on the meat. Then I looked Barry squarely in the eye. "I wasn't trying to get Mom angry, just you."

He did his Mr. Spock imitation with his eyebrow.

"I wanted you to be so mad at me that you'd hate my guts."

"What?" Mom said in a worried tone. "Why would you want that?"

I shook my head. "I'm not sure, but I think it has something to do with Barry moving in."

"Because I'm changing the life you have with your Mom?" Barry probed.

"No," I tried to explain. "Because I like you. And because I want you to be my dad. I want a father again." A large tear rolled out of my left eye and dripped onto my hamburger bun. It was followed by another large tear from my right eye. The tear tracks tickled my skin, and I shivered slightly.

Mom reached across the table and took my hand. "What are you trying to say, honey?"

"I'm not sure," I told them. "It was something Brent said the other day. Something about his stepmom. How he was afraid his dad would get divorced again. And it has something to do with how we worry about Grandpa." From the expressions on their faces, it was obvious my parents didn't understand what I was talking about.

"I loved Dad," I went on. "And when he died, it hurt so much. I don't ever want to hurt like that again." Mom squeezed my hand tighter. "I think I thought that if you didn't like me, Barry, then it wouldn't hurt so much if you left me because you and Mom didn't get along or if the same thing happened to you that happened to Dad." My vision was so blurry with tears, I couldn't see how Mom and Barry were reacting.

I felt Barry touch my other hand, and I quickly

grabbed his. "You guys really cut short your honeymoon to come home to see me?" I asked between my sobs.

"Of course," Mom said. And then she and Barry chorused, "We love you, Nicole."

"And I love you too," I cried.

✦ ✦ ✦

Brent came out to my farm with his dad the next day. While Mr. McGregor finished fixing the pool, I took Brent to my favorite spot by the creek. We sat on the grassy bank and watched a pair of squirrels chase each other through the branches of the aspens.

"So you're not grounded at all?" he asked.

"No," I told him. "My folks and I had a long talk. And we're going to keep talking. In fact, we're going to see someone in town and figure out how to make our new family work the best it can."

"A counselor?" Brent asked.

I nodded. "I still don't understand exactly what I'm feeling, and Barry thinks talking to someone else will help us learn to talk to each other better."

"Your dad sounds like a nice guy," Brent noted.

My dad, I thought. I wonder if I'll ever be able to call him Dad.

"Yeah, he is," I agreed.

"How are the cow and calf?" he wanted to know.

"Fine. Mom let them out in the pasture. We'll check on them later if you want. Brent has already grown a bit."

"How come you named a calf after me?" he wanted to know.

"Because he's so cute."

We both blushed when I said that.

"I'm really pleased your dad fixed the pool," I said to change the subject.

"He's good at that stuff," Brent said. Then he paused for a moment. "Would you like to go to a movie with me tonight?"

"Sure."

He smiled. "And maybe you can come into town every so often, and we can go to McDonald's and stuff."

I nodded. "Sure."

"That's great."

We smiled stupidly at each other for a few seconds. Finally, I worked up the courage to ask, "If we were in Toronto, would this mean we're going with each other?"

"Yeah," he said matter-of-factly and took my hand. "Let's go look for the cow and me."

We stood up.

"And after your dad finishes, we can fill up the

pool. It'll take a few hours, but maybe we'll have time for a swim."

"As long as you don't invite any cows to join us," he said.

Martyn Godfrey began his career as a junior high school teacher. He wrote his first book, a science fiction story, as a result of a deal he made with one of his students. It was published in 1981. He is now the author of more than 20 books, and has plans for at least that many more! Exciting and outrageous as his stories may be, Martyn says that they are generally inspired by actual events from the classroom or schoolyard.

Frank O'Keeffe is the author of *Guppy Love or The Day the Fish Tank Exploded* (Kids Can Press) and *School Stinks* (General). He was born in Dublin, Ireland. As a child, he won a prize for a story about survivors of a plane crash in South America, a place says he'd love to visit someday. He moved to Canada in 1957. When he's not writing, Frank spends his time teaching, raising cattle, and learning Spanish.

Printed in Canada